Long for More & More

Para Neyla
con mucho cariño
Doris Plummer

Doris Plummer

Long for More & More

ISBN: 978-958-49-1962-5

Corrections by Juan Fernando Merino

Text designed and typeset by Darlyn Vanessa Medina Valencia

Printed by Impre Libros – Cali, Colombia
The wording, style and content of this book is solely the responsibility of the author.
Impre Libros acts only as publisher.

Acknowledgements

I would like to thank my son Matthew Plummer for the amazing cover he designed for this book.

www.plummerfernandez.com

And Sebastian Kruk for taking a lovely picture of me.

www.sebkpotography.com
email: sebkphoto@gmail.com

And to all my friends that helped me through this amazing journey: Anabella Nader, Margota Cabrera, Sharon McGuire, Ruth Albañez, Monica Radcliffe, Ana Radcliffe, Mariela Angel, Beatriz Hall, Martha Bibby, Clara Zapata, Lucia Alvarez de Toledo, Nora Ohrenstein, Helga Marenda, Lola Serna, Yamila Borges, Patricia Gomez.

Long for More & More

How many times must I have my heart broken before I learn the lesson I am supposed to learn? Time after time, I fall for the wrong guy, and even though deep down I know I am doing it, I still bang my head against that brick wall. Goodness gracious, Gaby, wake up!!!; take a good look at yourself: you are a good-looking intelligent woman with lots to give, and yet, all you seem to want in life is a man with a pretty face and not much more to offer… So it should come as no surprise that soon after he tries this hot chocolate all he wants is to move on to his next prey.

I took a good look in the mirror and saw this stranger looking back at me, black hair sticking up, makeup running down her cheeks. I didn't recognize myself anymore; why on earth do I cry for a man that is not worth a penny? I must overcome this ridiculous tendency in my life, it's not them; it's ME. I look into my big brown eyes and swear to myself that before I even look at another man I must effect real change in my life. Say it Gaby, say it, loud and clear: "I swear by Almighty God that I will change within me, learn to love and accept myself just as I am before I set eyes on another man!" I started feeling better even as I was saying it, as if the penny had dropped; the lightbulb in my head was finally starting to shine again.

Come on, enough of feeling sorry for yourself, Gaby, get your leggings and training shoes on, let's get that blood pumping again, make that expensive gym subscription pay dividends. Exercise will help you physically and mentally and will boost your energy. Better to keep telling myself all the benefits before I turn round and hide back in bed.

"Good morning, Gaby, good to see you; it's been a while. Let's hope it's not just a new year's resolution and that you will visit us more often". "Can't promise you anything but I'll try", I said blushing slightly and went straight inside the gym. How long was it since I last came to this place? The gym had been completely renovated and I had not even noticed. The sight of all the machines was daunting but I just jumped on the treadmill and started walking, head up, feeling like I could walk to the moon and back; however after a few minutes I glanced at my fellow athletes on the machines next to mine and they were both half my age, running like gazelles, wearing tight leotards, with their narrow waistline in view. Straight away, I realized I was doing it again, putting myself down. Gaby you were absolutely stunning at their age and maybe didn't go to a gym because it was not the thing to do, but my God! did you had men turning their heads to look at you. At that moment I remembered walking in the streets of Rome back then and the way men were looking at me. And when I asked a police officer for help as I was lost and he said. "I finish work in a few minutes and then I'll take you to the end on the earth". I looked back at the gazelles and thought they would love to look as good as me in a few years.

Memories are great: better have lots of them and the more the merrier; when I'm dying I want to have lots of good memories and no regrets. I remember what Wayne Dyer used to say: "Don't die with the music still in your head!" So, I told myself, get back on track one step at a time. I am beautiful just as I am, I kept repeating over and over again as I was walking, until I got tired and could go on no more.

Monday morning and back to work. I was dreading it and just going in the tube was an uphill task. I kept hoping the train would break down or something extraordinary would happen to the busy London underground network. Just look at everyone, all glued to their mobiles trying to find God knows what, maybe a text from their loved ones: I checked mine right away, and zero messages, not even a PPI request.

I walked into my place of work; it was home away from home but I had been there far too long. I was a marketing director for an adverting company; things had changed over the years but not me. It had been difficult to keep up with technology but I still had a good eye for market trends, was good with clients and people found me reliable and trustworthy. How boring! But I just stayed and stayed.

"Morning, Gaby; how was your weekend?", Linda, my PA and good friend, said in her usual cheerful way. She had a rounded face, long hair, was just a bit on the chubby side, but always had the most beautiful smile.

"Don't even ask; Peter's hopped off to someone else's bed".

"I told you so! When are you going to stop going out with toy boys? They keep getting younger and younger: next you will be going out with someone younger than my sons. And don't even think about any of my boys; they are off your radar. You can do so much better than that", Linda said with quite a fuming tone of voice.

"Now, Linda; no need to get upset; getting annoyed with me isn't the answer. Let's go and make ourselves some coffee and calm down. I know I must change so you better use your energy to help me make a plan to fix me up".

First hurdle: I went back to my desk and started scrolling around the internet; I wanted to find a clinic to get a Botox treatment. Hmm, that would make me look so much better. I took some selfies on my mobile and started playing around with some apps. Oh, yes, if I straighten here and there, my God! I will look ten years younger, Fantastic!!!

I booked a clinic not too far so I could go after work, but at 5 o'clock Linda and some other colleagues were waiting for me at reception: "Come on Gaby; let's go and cheer you up down the Pub; a few Proseccos will clear your mind of any toy-boy past or present".

Oh, dear, I was not expecting this; not on a Monday evening, not the Pub!

"Not tonight; sorry, guys, but I have an appointment somewhere else".

"You haven't found another toy-boy on Tinder, have you?", asked Mark. "That was fast, even for you".

"No, nothing like that; I have a problem with my boiler and have booked a plumber to come and take a look before it does break down".

"OK, we will let you off the hook, but tomorrow prepare for a good night out".

That was close; I hurried out the door and vanished before they said anything else.

The clinic was just off Harley Street, very posh and absolutely packed —guess I am not the only one hoping for a quick fix— but I was surprised to find mostly young people there. I was expecting to see a load of middle age women wishing to get rid of a few wrinkles here and there but wasn't expecting to find a lot of young beautiful women unhappy with the way they looked. I started to talk to the girl next to me, a very pretty tall blond with legs that would go on forever.

"Hi, I'm Gaby; just wondering what brings you here; you look gorgeous to me".

"Hi. I am Ivanka; nice to meet you. I'm here for a couple of treatments. I want to get rid of a few wrinkles on my forehead and get bigger lips; you can never have lips big enough; men love big plump juicy lips", she said while trying to frown.

"I can't see any wrinkles on your forehead. How old are you?"

"I'm 28; and look here: you see", she said, pointing to the space between her eyebrows.

"You don't get wrinkles at 28; wait until you are my age".

I was looking closely at her, trying hard to see any wrinkles but at that moment the receptionist came out calling my name.

"Gaby, Gaby". I stood up and said good bye to Ivanka

"Hello, I'm Yvette; I'm the head esthetician in this clinic. Have you had any treatments before and what can I help you with today?"

Yvette was a very beautiful soft-spoken lady with skin like porcelain and not a wrinkle in sight.

"No, I haven't had any treatments before and by the look of all the young ladies in the waiting room it appears as if I was leaving it far too late".

"Never too late", replied Yvette smiling

"I would like to lose my winkles and get big plump juicy lips; in short, I want to look younger and feel better about myself".

"Leave it to me; I will have you looking like a teenager in no time".

After several painful needles had pricked my face, I was left with a few bruises, very swollen lips and a big dent in my bank account.

I called in sick for the next three days. Linda was very worried and I tried to reassure her that it was just the flu, pretending to have a sore throat and runny nose but on Friday I had to attend an important meeting so I covered all the bruises the best I could. Nevertheless the red swollen lips were there for all to see.

As soon as I walked in, Linda took a good look at me and burst out laughing, "I can see that the plumber wasn't exactly fixing the drains at home that evening. God, that looks painful!"

I went straight to the meeting and all the men were staring at my lips; they were either wondering what had happened to me or in fact all men like big fat juicy lips, as Ivanka had said.

At 5 o'clock, Linda and the office gang were waiting for me at reception. "Let's go and put those lips to the test; let's go and drink to them", said Mark, winking at me with a big smile.

We went to the French House in Soho's Dean Street. It was packed as usual; we stayed there laughing and having some pub food; everyone made jokes about my cold and the plumbing but around 9 everyone went back home and I just didn't want to be at home on my own. I decided to go to Ronnie Scotts; Fridays is the Latin night "Viva Cuba" at the place. I love salsa dancing and it is a place where people just go to dance and it actually feels as if you are in a night club in Havana. The place was as vibrant as usual, packed with Cuban men wanting to dance and flirt with the local girls; I danced and drank maybe a bit too much.

The following morning, I was woken up by the sweet voice of a black man lying naked next to me. "Hola, Bonita", he said.

I jumped out of bed horrified to find a total stranger next to me. "How on earth did you get here?" Without waiting for a reply, I locked myself in the bathroom and took a long shower, as if I wanted to wash any trace of the man in my body. I put on my bathrobe and when I opened the door, he had vanished, probably too scared by my reaction, or maybe by the sight of the not so "bonita" lady he had been in bed with.

I sat on my bed in disbelief of what had happened. I had fucked a man I would not be able to recognize even if I walked pass him on the street. What was I doing to myself? What was wrong with me? One thing was very clear: this was not the change that I needed in my life right now; trying to change the way I looked was not making me feel better about myself. I had to change within me. I started searching the internet; there must be a talk or a workshop that could help me out; after all, I live in London where everything happens, for any taste and need. I just wrote on the browser of my laptop "self-help talks" and a long list of events appeared on my screen. A few were sold out, but some still had places available.

Let's see: Davidji "Meditations to change your Brain". That sounded quite appropriate. I could definitely do with a new brain. "Shift Happens", talk by Robert Holden, also sounds interesting. I needed a complete overhaul… "Dying to be Me" by Anita Moorjani, "My Journey from Cancer, to Near Death to True Healing". I kept reading about her and although I didn't have a life threatening illness, (although if I were to continue on this path I could end up killing myself), her story and her recovery sounded very interesting. I booked a ticket before I had time to change my mind.

The talk was taking place at Regent's Park University, a lovely campus in the middle of the park; the place was almost full but I managed to get an empty seat right at the front of the conference room. A very sweet middle age Indian lady appeared on stage; she told her story about how she became so obsessed with cancer after her father and her best friend had both succumbed to the illness that she had made herself ill, about all her experiences during her illness and how she died and came back to tell her story about the power of our thoughts and that above all we should love ourselves unconditionally. She asked everyone in the audience to write something good about him or herself. I kept staring at my blank piece of paper but could not come up with anything good to say about me. Anita then asked the audience if there was anyone that could not find anything good about themselves and I was the only one to raise the hand. She looked at me and asked me to go up the stage with her. She then asked everyone to say nice things about me and I was surprised to hear all the lovely things that people were shouting; tears started rolling down my cheeks, she gave me a signed copy of her book and told me to go and live my life fearlessly.

I stayed in bed all day on Sunday reading her book. I was surprised to find out that she was "discovered" by Wayne Dyer and his words kept resounding on my brain: "Don't die with the music still in your head".

I looked at myself in my good old friend, the mirror. "Gaby is time for you to do all those things you have always dreamt of doing but always kept finding excuses not to do".

First thing Monday morning I went straight to my boss's office. "Tom, I'm handing in my resignation".

"Wait a minute, wait a minute; what's gone into your head?; you can't resign just like that", Tom said, pulling himself back. My words had taken him completely by surprise. Tom was in his late fifties, his hair was thinning a bit but he still looked attractive. He had built this company from scratch, pouring his heart and soul into it and he had seen me do the same and I knew he considered me one of his best employees.

"Listen, Tom; I am going through a middle age crisis; don't think for a minute that women don't go through them the same as men; the only thing I haven't done and only because I can't afford it is buy a Lamborghini. I desperately need a change; I have been here far too long and can't keep going anymore". I was begging Tom to let me go.

"Why don't you take a 6 months sabbatical and after that time if you still want to leave, I will accept your resignation, but please don't go until you find a replacement", said a fairly relieved Tom.

"No need to find one. Linda my PA knows the company inside out and is very familiar with all the accounts I handle. The clients know her well too and she deserves a promotion; so it's a win-win substitution".

Tom stood up and gave me a big hug while whispering in my ear "Please come back; there will always be a place for you here".

The next few weeks were very hectic; I had deals to finish at work while preparing Linda to step into my shoes. I put all my personal belongings in storage so I could rent my flat and generate income for my sabbatical and I was also training really hard at the gym. I had decided that I would start by walking the Camino de Santiago, or the Way of Saint James, a grueling 800-kilometer pilgrimage that would take me over a month to walk. Many people have walked it, St. Francis of Assisi, Paulo Coelho, Shirley MacLaine, Sonia Choquette, and the millions of pilgrims that walk it every year.

The Camino

So here I am in a flight heading towards the Camino, with my rucksack, sleeping bag, a few possessions and a lucky scarf to keep me company during this pilgrimage.

As I was staring out the window, looking at the clouds passing by, I started talking to myself: "Good, at long last you took the plunge, Gaby; it took you a long time to finally get here; it's about time that you finally began doing something for yourself, although walking around 30 kilometres a day for over a month is not exactly pampering; it is more like cruelty than love but it's good to finally start playing the songs in your head and begin living. And what I mean by living is not just breathing, or working and paying the bills, but actually taking time to look and be aware of everything around you".

After a long journey by plane, bus and train, I found myself standing at the station in St Jean Pied de Port, the beginning of my pilgrimage and of this great journey. There were quite a few pilgrims coming out of the train and into the platform; we just looked and smiled at each other not knowing what to do.

Once I found an albergue to spend the night, I went to the passport office to get my pilgrim passport with my first stamp on it and a scallop shell to put on my rucksack. And so I became an official pilgrim ready to start the Camino. The passport is very important as it allows you to identify yourself as a pilgrim, gets you good discounts in restaurants and also allows you to stay in the albergues. You have to collect stamps from every place, bar, albergue, town hall you pass by as in Santiago they will check it as proof that you walked it all the way, before they give you the Compostela certificate of completion of the Camino de Santiago, issued to you by the Pilgrim's Office in Santiago de Compostela.

I went to walk around the town, a very beautiful petite French village on the foothills of the Pyrenees, with a river crossing it and very steep roads; at one point I saw a church and was drawn to it. As I walked in and stood in front of a statue of the Virgin Mary I just started crying, and not just crying: I let go of all the burdens of life, all the sorrows, all that had been keeping me from moving on. It was as if a veil had been lifted from my soul. I did not even know why I was crying but I just did. After a while I let go and started finding peace within me. I finally came out of the church and made my way around the town full of pilgrims, anxiously waiting to start the Camino.

I quietly sneaked out of the albergue before dawn the next morning, and as I walked down the narrow streets of the village, I could see many pilgrims looking for the distinctive yellow arrows and shells that would show us the way throughout our journey, "Buen Camino". I held my scarf close to me. Finally,

Gaby; here we go taking this very important step to follow my dreams in this journey called life.

The first day is like learning how to walk again. There is no car, no train, no bus, just a good pair of walking boots, and your rucksack. As the day went by I started to realize how heavy those few possessions really were and how travelling light is the key to everything; we need so little and yet we try and fill our lives with things we don't need, thinking they will make us happy, when freedom is all we wish for. I started meeting people, the ones that would be my companions. Some of them would be there for a few days and then we would meet up again further along the way; some others would be my friends throughout the journey and still others will show up just when we need them the most, when we need a push, a helping hand, a friend to laugh, to cry with and enjoy a good meal, a glass of wine, a friend to talk to...a friend to walk with and know that he is there walking next to us not saying anything but just knowing that he is there. I realized how important friends are, how I long to find that someone that is there for me, at the other end of the phone, at the centre of my heart.

Right in the middle of the mountains, while I was having a rest and enjoying the majestic views of the Pyrenees, basking in the beauty of my surroundings, I saw a guy desperately trying to get a signal on his mobile phone.

"I don't think you will get a signal here; we are crossing the border and up here I doubt if they even know what a mobile looks like".

"But I must; I have a very important deal to close and I will never forgive myself if I miss this opportunity". A frantic guy wearing matching shoes and rucksack full of trendy accessories screamed back at me.

"I am sure that when you die you won't forgive yourself for not making that call or making that "big" deal, but I am absolutely sure that you won't forgive yourself for not taking notice of this beautiful mountains, or not listening to the song of the birds or the jingle in your soul".

He looked at me as if I was the craziest woman on earth and just kept searching for that elusive signal out there, where there was no way to be found. We always are trying to search for that elusive something that we think will make us happy; its like a mirage you keep trying to search for, something that doesn't exist, like when you go to a fridge thinking you will find happiness eating whatever is inside but when you open that door of course you don't. We keep looking everywhere when happiness is looking at us right in front of our nose, deep down inside us.

I arrived at Roncesvalles absolutely exhausted. I booked a bed in the Collegiate Monastery and had my first taste of proper communal sleeping, as the Monastery sleeps 180 people all under the beautiful roof of the 13th century building. I looked at the big hall full of bunkbeds and searched for a bed; the only ones left were at the top. I looked at the ladders; God you are joking; I am so tired I will not be able to climb up there; it looks just like Mount Everest. Finally I grabbed the ladder and jumped up to my bed and what seemed like landing right in heaven; up there I could listen to the murmur of all the pilgrims, some snoring quite loud, and I just thought I would never be able to fall asleep, but I was so tired that as soon as I hit the pillow I was gone. I had the most amazing vivid dreams; I felt as my spirit lifted out my body and I met up with relatives and friends that had already passed away: I could just make up their faces, all happy to see me and cheering me up: "don't give up, don't give up, just keep going no matter what". I slowly landed back into my body, and as I tried to move my legs, they would not respond, they were aching all over. I just looked up to the sky and said quietly...no wonder you were cheering me up, but to be honest I don't think I can go on, I can't move. I started listening to the other pilgrims waking up and moaning and hearing all complain about the aches and pains, and slowly started putting my boots back on and made my way down to the cafe.

I needed a strong black coffee, hoping that the caffeine would give me a jump-start. As the lady behind the counter poured my cup of coffee she looked at me and said: "It does get easier; your legs will get used to the long walks and the rucksack and at the end of your journey, once you reach Santiago, you will miss it all, so just enjoy it. Today is an easier day, no steep mountains to climb, but very beautiful, just keep going. Buen Camino".

It was so good just being out there, enjoying nature and talking to other people; some walked in groups or with their family but most of all we walked on our own, wanting to connect back to life and forget about work and problems and headaches, trying to find out who we really are, where we are and why are we here. Making sure that we walked back to heaven and not get lost in the labyrinth of life.

I stopped to have breakfast at a lively café in the next village. I sat in a table and after a few minutes, a good-looking guy asked me if he could share my table, as the café was now full.

"Please, go ahead; I'm just waiting for my breakfast. I'm starving; it must be all the walking and fresh air", I said pointing at a chair in front of me.

"Hello, I'm George, nice to meet you. Are you walking alone?", he asked with a soft Irish accent.

"Hi, I am Gaby; yes, I am walking alone but as you can see there are plenty of us pilgrims so not really lonely; actually I didn't realize it was going to be this busy", I replied blushing a bit; it was a bit daunting to meet someone early in the morning wearing zero makeup and very unattractive clothes.

"The Camino is a special place, is not a mere coincidence that so many people have walked it throughout the years. The Camino follows the Milky Way and it's a place where magic happens, a path that will help you start to understand yourself and show you the way towards discovering heaven on earth".

"That sounds very profound but it does feel quite special to be here".

"I have walked it a few times; it's really magical".

As I stood up to continue walking, Gorge said to me.

'The Camino doesn't give you what you want; it gives you what you need, as life does".

I winked back at him and kept on walking.

As I reached Pamplona, I realized it was just three days before the fiestas of San Fermin, so the city was packed with tourists, and wannabe bull runners. Thank God I was staying at the Municipal Albergue of Jesús y Maria, which is reserved only for pilgrims; otherwise, I would not have found a place to sleep. I went out that evening and soon got caught out in the partying, dancing and laughing. I saw George and as soon as he saw me, he walked straight to me.

"You look gorgeous!" he said.

Thanks, but this is the only dress I have besides my hiking clothes".

"Good; that means you don't have to take ages every evening standing in front of your wardrobe not knowing what to wear".

"That's exactly what I do", I replied laughing.

We danced all night long on the streets of Pamplona, carefree, just listening to the music, hoping that it would never end, but end it did and next day having to walk again with a hangover and having slept very little was quite painful. A voice in my head just kept going on and on: "Don't give up, don't give up". I focused on my next stage "Puente la Reina". I wanted to spend the night at Paulo Coelho's albergue and meet him, as apparently he often spent many evenings there greeting pilgrims, giving words of hope and wisdom. I also wanted to thank him for his books and for inspiring me to walk this Camino. Having a focus kept me going all day; I cannot remember a lot of that stage; I only wanted to arrive. Once I was approaching the albergue, I saw Viviane, a very beautiful blond young Brazilian with whom I had walked a few times, looking quite gloomy. He was not there and the place was already full. I nearly collapsed; I was so much looking forward to this albergue and was so totally exhausted that I just wanted to cry. My friend looked at me... We have to keep going as at this late in the afternoon there won't be many beds left in any of the albergues, she told me. And so we walked on to the next one and the next and everything was full. It seemed that as Pamplona was so busy, people had walked the extra mile and everything in Puente la Reina was gone, so we just kept walking and on the road we saw a sign, "Casa Rural" rooms available. We took the small path that looked quite spooky, but as we were so tired and had no other option, we kept walking and it led us to the most enchanting country cottage, with a stream running in front of it and hanging baskets with the most amazing colourful flowers. I knocked at the door and a very charming lady opened; she said that as it was quite late, she didn't think any more pilgrims would turn up so we could have a room each and she offered to wash all our dirty clothes. As we waited for our meal, a delicious home cooked dinner made just for us, we put our tired feet on the cold stream. It was pure bliss!

Finally, I went back to my room...did I say it co-rrectly? "My own room", just for myself, no noise, no snoring, no pilgrims talking...Heaven! I collapsed into my bed and I remembered what George had said: "The Camino always gives you what you need, not exactly what you want". I wondered what had happened to George; I had not seen him all day during the walk; maybe he had stayed in Pamplona partying.

The following morning, after having a scrumptious breakfast and with a rucksack full of clean clothes, my friend and I started to walk along the small path to re-join the Camino. Once we reached it, we tried to find the sign that we had seen the night before, indicating us the way to the cottage and only after moving some branches, we found the small sign, "Casa Rural, Rooms Available". We looked at each other and wondered how on earth we had seen it the previous evening, and after debating whether to put it or not in a more prominent position, we left it there, where it was probably intended to be, so that pilgrims in great need could spend a night in heaven.

I felt the breeze touching my face; I just wanted to walk in silence, enjoying my own company, just taking it all in and paying full attention to my surroundings. This must be the real mindfulness that is so trendy now and yet so simple. I was beginning to feel the peacefulness that I was so much yearning for. The stress of a deadline, the mobile ringing, the crowded trains and the anxiety to fit in society were starting to fade away.

I was walking next to Vivian and yet we said nothing to each other, just giving ourselves time and space to experience just being there. Most of the time people chatter so much, and no one pays any attention to each other; sometimes is best not to say anything but really listen to each other's soul.

Why had I made life so difficult and complicated for myself when it could be so simple? I'm sure God never intended life to be such a struggle and yet there is so much suffering. I think it's important for everyone to start walking back to heaven, life is meant to be enjoyed, we want so much and yet we only need very little to be truly happy. We must wake up to this reality and change that old paradigm of hardship, sin and suffering, that has always been used to control us by religions, governments, school, parents, partners, bosses, you name it!. Once everyone realizes this, doors will start opening for all; there is plenty for all on this beautiful earth; just look around you, Gaby; you are already walking in heaven; only you just had not realized it or noticed it before.

Talking about paradise, I saw a spring made in heaven, the famous Irache wine fountain, which has two taps; one dispenses wine and the other fresh water. There were several pilgrims filling the water bottles with wine. I just went there and drank some straight from the tap; I closed my eyes and enjoyed every drop of it!

I kept on walking for a few days, talking to pilgrims, passing by many villages with the most amazing churches. Spain is such a beautiful country and people are so nice, welcoming all the pilgrims and just saying the usual encouraging words, "Buen Camino".

I arrived at Burgos, were I was meeting up with a fried that had flown from afar; she was booked in a boutique hotel, a far cry from the albergues I had been staying at. There was even a hair dryer in the bathroom, total luxury, and I was taken aback by the amount of baggage she had brought with her. "I soon had to phone and arrange for rucksack van carriers: there are all options available in the Camino, just in case you can't cope and this pilgrim helpers have become big business,".

Burgos is a city brimming with majestic architecture and was home to the notorious El Cid. My friend and I went for a walk along the river and through the narrow streets of the city. The gothic style cathedral was amazing but the Saint Nicholas de Bari church built by merchants, with its stunning altar, took my breath away. I felt at home, as if I had already been there, and as I sat to pray, I noticed the number 44 scribbled on the bench. The number 44 is known as the Angel Number and when it appears, it indicates that you are being surrounded by loving angels and given support and encouragement along your path and that is exactly how I felt.

As we started walking along the Camino I soon realized that me and my friend were in two very different mind frames; she was more interested in meeting the handsome men along the Camino and looking good with all the clothes she had brought with her than really enjoying the scenery; however, as she was there only for a few days I thought it was best to seize the moment and go along with it. At the next big town I bought some new clothes and went to the hairdressers to have my hair done; everyone in the Camino noticed it and they all started making jokes about my new dress and new look. We started drinking more wine and sharing more with other pilgrims, and to my surprise, I was enjoying every minute of it. As we sat in one of the cafes in a small village, we overheard a group of middle age matrons plotting to follow the butcher's wife, as they were sure she was having an affair with a man in a village nearby. It was the best ever soap opera we have ever heard. And we were also plotting to see how one of us was going to catch a German guy that was the most gorgeous pilgrim in the whole Camino. It was a week of pure girls' fun that went by really quick and then we parted in Leon; she headed back home and me back to walking by myself and carrying my rucksack.

Oh, dear; that rucksack felt really heavy. I was not used to it anymore and with those extra clothes I had bought it felt as if I was carrying stones. And then I heard a voice asking me: "Can I help you with that?" It was George with a big grin on his face.

"Hello, stranger; I thought you had stayed in Pamplona. I never saw you again"

"I did stay a couple of extra days; it was a lot on fun but since then I have been walking quite fast trying to catch up with you".

"Have you?" I asked quite surprised.

"You left and I don't even have your number or have any idea where you live and haven't got a clue as to how to contact you; so yes, I have walked really fast", George said looking directly into my eyes.

I don't think I've ever had a man walking fast just to catch up with me. He looked genuinely interested in me and it felt good; he liked me just as I was, no makeup, no stilettoes, just plain me and it felt good.

"I live in London, close to Bayswater tube station, in a ground floor flat with a small garden, that is currently let out as I have taken a six-month sabbatical", I said to George while I started walking again. Somehow the rucksack felt light and I was feeling very energized.

"I live quite close, in Notting Hill, and one of my daughters is looking after my flat".

My heart suddenly stopped. "So you are married?" I asked, sounding very disappointed.

"Divorced. And you?"

"Married to my job, but hoping to get a divorce when I get back. I have never married; I am an only child and have always find it difficult to share my life with anyone. How many kids do you have?"

"I have two daughters that can't make up their minds as weather to live with me or their mother; she remarried and has a baby boy, with another one on the way. She is much younger than me".

"So, you were replaced for a younger guy. Welcome to the club. I thought it only happened to us women". Somehow that made me feel elated and I started walking a bit faster as if to prove the point that I still had it in me, but he soon caught up with me. "You are not going to lose me this fast", he said.

I smiled back and felt really happy.

Late that afternoon we reached Astorga, a beautiful town that has an amazing neo-Gothic Bishop's Palace designed by Antonio Gaudi; the whole place just looks like a film set.

As we went into the albergue the man at the reception desk asked "passports please?" I handed in my pilgrim passport. "Your country passport too, please". I looked at George just next to me and handed in my UK passport. The man looked at the passport, looked at me and asked "Date of birth?" I swallowed hard and said it out loud. That was it; I had said it; now it was all out in the open, I would not have to lie about my age. The man at the reception looked at George "You too, sir; passport please", and before he was even asked, he said his birth date. He was three years younger than me. Not exactly a toy boy, I said to myself, smiling.

I slept in the top bunk bed, I kept piping from the side of my bed: first time I had slept on top of a man without touching him, but I quickly turned round an fell asleep. I don't think I had ever slept so good, not only because I was so damn tired but due to the lack of worries and anxiety.

I woke up early, as I wanted to get out of bed and at least wash my face and clean up before George woke up, but in spite of all my best efforts as soon as I started climbing down the ladders, I heard his voice. "Good morning, gorgeous". There was no place to hide; I thought about jumping back in my sleeping bag but could not do so I just gave him my best smile and quickly made a run for the bathroom.

He was waiting for me at the cafeteria with a big cup of coffee ready for me.

From then on is a steep climb until you reach The Cruz del Ferro, an iron cross on top of a 5-metre wooden pole. There you are supposed to leave a stone as sign of leaving behind your "old" life, and so becoming lighter both physically and spiritually. I had brought with me a small crystal and I left it amongst the many thousands of stones already there. It is quite an emotional moment, as most pilgrims take their time to reflect about what they are leaving behind and the sobbing is quite contagious. I reflected on my life and thought about all the things that had helped me reach this point in my life. All the silly things I had clung to that didn't really matter much. After all we come to this world naked and we leave it the same way; all that counts is our memories, like walking this Camino. Just being there in front of that tall cross reminded me that letting go was far better that holding on.

George was there also submersed in his own thoughts; we gave each other space and time before starting the descent and on the way down somehow I lost sight of him. If I thought going up the hill was hard going down was even worse, my knees were feeling it and my legs had to exercise muscles that had never been used before. I began inquiring about a place to stay and could not find any. I was getting quite desperate and started to cry; was it all worth it? And then one of the pilgrim "helpers" vans passed me by and as they saw me crying, they stopped and asked if I needed help.

"I am tired, desperate and can't find a place to stay the night", I retorted, looking really sorry for myself. "Come on, jump in, we are going to deliver some rucksacks in a very nice private albergue; it even has a swimming pool and it overlooks the Templar's Castle in Ponferrada". I looked at the number plates of the van and it ended in 44 and just thought that true angels had been sent to my rescue. "This place is a bit off the route of the Camino so it doesn't get that busy, and tomorrow morning when we come to collect the rucksacks will drop you back in the Camino", said the driver. Soon enough we arrived at the albergue. Wow, what a view of the castle!; it was lovely. The driver winked at me and said: "Trust the Camino; it has its own way of making sure that pilgrims arrive safely all the way to Santiago... Buen Camino; see you tomorrow".

I went straight to the swimming pool; it was such a lovely warm summer evening, with a view of the Templar's Castle and a full moon. What else could I ask for? My legs started to feel better relaxing in the water and as I looked up, I saw the most beautiful full moon rising in the sky. I wondered where George had gone and as I still had not given him my mobile number, there was no way he could contact me.

Early next morning the van was waiting for me to take me back to the Camino trail and they offered to take my rucksack to an albergue in Villafranca, the next stage in the Camino, an offer I could not refuse after the hardships of the previous day. I could really do with a day walking light. The day went really quick; this stage is very pleasant and not very demanding, so I arrived to the albergue very early, in fact too early as it was closed. I could see my rucksack already inside but the door was locked, a bit of a shame as I always liked to take a shower as soon as I arrived. I was standing there by the door not knowing what to do when a bystander asked me if I needed any help. I explained what had happened and he suggested that I should knock in the house next-door, as the lady there offered really good feet massages to pilgrims.

I pressed the doorbell and after a few minutes a very petite lady with a broad smile opened the door. "Please come in; I am Carmen; make yourself at home while I go to make us some coffee". I was a bit taken aback to see someone welcoming into their home without even asking me a single question. The house was a little bit spooky; it smelled of incense and was full of religious ornaments and Christian pictures on the walls, a bit over the top and rather dark, and then for a minute I questioned myself if I should be in there at all.

"Come on, relax", said the lady when she came into the lounge holding two cups of coffee; "you need a good rest after a long day walking; put your feet up and later on I can give you a good relaxing massage, to help you ease all the pain in those poor feet".

I immediately felt at ease; she had a soothing tone of voice and there was something very special about her. She kept smiling and looking at me. She then said. "I knew you were coming; sometimes I wake up with this feeling that I can't leave home until that someone special arrives, and as soon as I opened the door, I knew that the person I was waiting for was you".

"Well, let me tell you I am not a VIP".

"I am never wrong. Have you finished drinking your coffee?" And as I gave her my empty cup, she turned the cup upside down on the plate, she waited a few minutes, then lifted the cup and had some coffee sediment on the plate. She kept staring at it, nodding, humming. Then she looked at me. "Interesting life you've had, but don't know what you want yet, its good you are walking The Camino; it will show you the way, but remember reaching Santiago is not important, it's the journey itself, just like your path on this earth, right now, make it count, make it a good one. You came here for a purpose, you must help people wake up, but before you do so, you must start by waking up yourself".

I was gobsmacked: You can see all that from some coffee sediment?"

"Well, I can see all about your life. I can also tell you that you are not walking alone; you have a very special companion and he can help you in this life if you let him; he is a very special soul, ask him; I've had him sitting right in front of me on a couple of occasions. He is a seeker, just like you".

"Oh well, right now I've lost him, and I don't have his number or anything, I can't even remember his surname".

"Trust me, you will meet again. You see, I was waiting for you; I am never wrong".

"And I thought I was coming here for a foot massage".

I had so many questions I wanted to ask her but she ushered me to the door, and explained that she had said all she needed to tell me... "Buen Camino".

I went back to the albergue, now open. I took my rucksack and headed straight to the shower. I stayed there letting the cold water clear my head and soothe my body, I was on a daze, not quite knowing what to make up of what had just happened.

I woke up early the following day; I had heard that the climb to O Cebreiro was the hardest of all of the Camino; there are a few places that you can stay along the way but I really wanted to make it all the way there. The O Cebreiro hamlet lies at the top of the mountain; there is a chapel dedicated to Saint Francis of Assisi and some say that he received one of his stigmata when he reached the top and some even say that the challis on the chapel was the one that Jesus used during his last supper. I walked all day by myself; I really wanted to be on my own, taking in all the experiences that I had so far in the Camino and in my life. I was realizing how amazing life is and how wonderful is this earth, how perfect is the human body, how I can move, and breath, I have no idea how, but it just does and it's perfect, and maybe this could be heaven and we are just missing out. We lose ourselves in the daily routine trying to make a living but not actually enjoying the ride. I thought about earth and how we humans have been trying so hard to destroy it. I just looked at the scenery and took a deep breath in and I just felt wonderful, but as I looked up I could hardly see the top of the mountain and I knew that if I wanted to reach it I had to make a big effort and keep going. I started singing and watching everything around me, somehow I felt that I was being helped and pushed and before I knew I was there at the top. I went straight to the chapel; mass was about to begin and the priest started by reading Saint Francis prayer:

Lord, make me an instrument of Your peace. Where there is hatred, let me sow love; where there is injury, pardon; where there is doubt, faith; where there is despair, hope; where there is darkness, light; where there is sadness, joy.

O, Divine Master, grant that I may not so much seek to be consoled as to console; to be understood as to understand; to be loved as to love; For it is in giving that we receive; it is in pardoning that we are pardoned; it is in dying that we are born again to eternal life.

I could feel tears rolling down my cheeks. What beautiful and meaningful prayer, what a great man! And to think that he had walked the same Camino all those years ago made me feel humble; the energy was so vibrant, I was so very grateful for being there, for being alive, for walking the Camino and walking on this earth right at that moment.

A couple of days later I arrived in Sarria, the last 100 kilometres before reaching Santiago and the minimum number of kilometres that one has to walk to be granted a Compostela certificate to say that you have walked the Camino. The following day there were hundreds of pilgrims; it felt like being in the rush hour back home. I never saw George again and wandered if what Carmen has said was actually true. I lost sight of most of the friends and somehow it was not the same. I had been warned about it and I had booked places to stay for the last five remaining days as the albergues get full very quickly and are not great, so I just walked and walked. By this stage all I wanted to do was to reach Santiago, arrive home: I was beginning to get tired of all the walking. I somehow compared it to old age; that is how it must feel when we are on the last stretch and all we want to do is to make it back home. Just before reaching Santiago there is the Mount of Joy and I could feel that happiness of nearly being there after more than one-month walking. I felt proud of all that I had achieved. My job, my flat, my friends back in London felt like such a distant memory, that I didn't think that after this pilgrimage I could go back there and sit back at my desk. I decided there and then that when I got back I would hand Tom my resignation, but that was still a long way away as I still had another few months before heading back to London and for now I had to concentrate on reaching Santiago.

Nothing can compare to the feeling of the moment when you first have a glimpse of that Cathedral, I had done it, all the walking, all the experiences. I just stood there by the entrance; then I went inside and knelt before the tomb of Saint James and thanked him, and as I walked by the front of the altar trying to find a place to sit I saw George: there was an empty place right next to him as if he were waiting for me. I sat there; neither of us said anything. The pilgrims mass was starting with the launch of the 'Botafumeiro', a huge incense burner that dates back to 1851 and is made of silver-plated brass. Eight men, called 'tiraboleiros', are needed to operate the 'Botafumeiro'. After being filled with incense and coal by the 'tiraboleiros', the 'Botafumeiro' is tied to a rope hanging by the altar and set in motion, forming an impressive arched trajectory along the cathedral that is meant to clean the pilgrim's souls. After that, all the names of the pilgrims that had made it to the cathedral are read aloud. I felt so proud to hear my name. Wow! I had made it to heaven and I was sitting next to George.

When we came out of the cathedral, we went to get our Compostela Certificates. We did not say much; it was a funny feeling and a very proud moment. As we came out George said.

"Now give me your number. I think I have earned it; I am heading back to London later on this afternoon, I hope I can call you and we can go out on a proper dinner close to home".

"You are leaving today?"

"Unfortunately yes, but I hope we can meet again soon"

"I won't be back in London for quite some time. Remember I told you I am on a six-month sabbatical; right now I'm heading to Málaga to spend some time with a friend and for a much-needed rest and then I am not sure".

"Then I'll be waiting for you in six months".

We gave each other a big hug; as he boarded the taxi, I could feel a tear rolling down my cheek and I realized we had not even kissed.

I spent a few days walking around Santiago, while deciding exactly what to do next. I saw most of my friends from the Camino; it was nice to catch up; we were talking in one of the bars and Vivian the Brazilian said she was going to Fátima, in Portugal.

"Are you going to walk all the way there? Are you doing the Portuguese Camino?"

"I'm going to follow it but by train and buses and from Portugal I will fly back to Rio", said Vivian very enthusiastically.

"Do you mind if I join you?; It would be great; I've always wanted to go to Fátima".

"That's absolutely fabulous. I didn't really want to travel on my own, it looks like the Camino is still working its magic!"

"When do we leave?"

"Tomorrow morning; the train leaves at 8am"

"I'll meet you at the station". I kissed and hugged everyone goodbye

Fátima

Vivian was waiting for me at the ticket office in the train station.

"Where shall I buy a ticket to?"

"Ourense"

We boarded a small local train that went quite slowly around the mountains; it was quite relaxing to be on a train and not walking, although I did miss it all.

"Why Ourense?" I asked Vivian.

"I have a friend that lives there; he is a homeopathy doctor and I have an appointment to see him tomorrow. You can also come if you want to"

"Are you ill?"

"Not really, but he twists my energy chakras and helps me out with anxiety. I am not sure exactly what he does but I always come out feeling much better; he is Brazilian but he moved there a couple of years ago; as I am so close, I couldn't miss seeing him".

"That sounds very interesting; let's hope he can see me too".

"His name is Roberto; he told me Ourense is a Roman mediaeval city with a lot of history and that there are some wonderful thermal spring waters. I think we can both spend some time relaxing in thermal waters"

"That sounds lovely and I'm sure they will have massages and treatments. I'm already dreaming about the pampering and a glass of the wonderful Albariño wine from Galicia".

Then the announcement came: "Next stop Ourense".

"That was quick". It took less than an hour to get there and after having to walk for hours to get anywhere during the Camino a short train journey to get to another town seemed incredible.

We went to the tourist office to try to find a place to stay; the lady behind the counter saw our rucksacks and shells and asked if we were pilgrims; we told her that we had just finished and that we were on our way to Fátima, but we were not walking anymore.

"Don't worry, show me your pilgrim passports and I will stamp it; you still get good discounts and are allowed to stay in the albergues; just keep having your passport stamped whenever you can".

She found us a room in a private albergue in the centre of town and after leaving our rucksacks there, we went straight to the springs. We had to board a small tourist train in front of the 12th-century Cathedral with its beautiful ornate Gate of Paradise. The train went along the medieval town, then crossed the iconic Roman bridge, with its trademark arches and on to the medicinal springs along the river.

"Which one do we go to?" I asked Vivian, realizing there were quite a few springs

"I have no idea", said Vivian with a confused look

"The Burga de Abajo", said the man sitting next to us. "Sorry, my name is Manuel, I overheard you talking; the Burga de Abajo is probably the nicest spring: there are several pools and they have a spa centre and you can choose a selection of therapies and massages. I am going there myself so I can show you".

"I am Vivian and this is my friend Gaby; nice to meet you", said Vivian shaking his hand

"That sounds great, Manuel; you speak very good English", I said to this muscular young man with a tan complexion.

"I went to the university in Manchester, but couldn't get used to the weather so I came back home".

"I agree with you regarding the British weather; I don't think I could get used to it. Being from Rio I adore the sun; it can never be too hot for me"

"This is our stop", said Manuel

We got off the train and we went down a steep trail until we reached a small kiosk; Vivian and I kept looking at each other, the place looked rather uninviting and it smelled of rotten eggs. However, when we got out of the small changing room, the door lead to the most spectacular set of bubbling hot pools. Nevertheless, the smell was still awful.

Manuel came out and as if reading our minds said: "Don't worry about the smell; is the sulphur in the water and all the healing minerals; you'll soon get used to it, I promise you that; just get in and think of all the goodness you are soaking in".

I looked at Manuel in his swimming trunks, OMG! What a body, what a temptation! Gaby please behave yourself, I told myself; he is very young and no, you are not here for another one-night stand… better concentrate only on the therapeutic waters.

The sensation of getting in the water is indescribable; it is so soothing and yes, you do forget about the awful smell. We found out that most of the people there were pilgrims on their way to Santiago coming from Fátima; we talked to them, all eager to reach Santiago. After spending all afternoon in the springs Vivian and I treated ourselves to a massage; afterwards we were sitting at the bar drinking a Spanish Cava, when Manuel came rushing in,

"Sorry, girls, but we have to go now; the last train leaves in 10 minutes and it's very difficult to get any other transport from here".

We gulped down our drinks and ran up the hill to the train stop; once in the train I thanked Manuel for taking us to that place. "I don't think we would have found those springs by ourselves; they are not the obvious first choice".

"Glad you liked them. How about going for a drink tonight? There is a street full of tapa bars; let me show you in the map". As he pointed the name of the street, we realized it was just around the corner from the place we were staying.

"See you at 10pm" said Manuel as he got off the train.

"I forget how late Spaniards go out to eat and drink,

we better get a nap before we go out tonight and set the alarm; I am so relaxed, I could sleep forever", I told Vivian.

Vivian looked at me with a horror expression on her face. "How are we going out tonight? We don't have any clothes to wear and hardly any makeup".

"Don't panic. I have a couple of dresses we can wear and you don't need makeup; you look amazing just as you are".

Later on we went out to look for Manuel; the bars were full of people and Manuel was nowhere to be seen; we ordered a couple of glasses of wine and stood outside the bar. After a good long half hour had gone by Manuel came up the road, wearing a pair of tight jeans and a black T-shirt that made him look even hotter that on his swimming trunks.

"Sorry I am late, girls; I was putting the children to sleep and it took me longer than usual".

"You are married", we shouted in unison

Manuel just gave us a big broad smile

"There is a saying in Spanish: "Hombre casado ni frito ni asado" "Married man neither fried nor roasted", said a rather annoyed Vivian. We finished our drinks and went back to bed.

The following morning, we woke up early as we were going to see Roberto; Vivian had managed to secure an appointment for me after hers. We arrived at a block of flats and after ringing the bell, a rather pleasant tall man with grey hair opened the door. "You must be Gaby", said Roberto, giving me a scanning look from head to toes. "Do you mind waiting at the coffee shop across the road; I don't like someone else's energy interfering with the client I'm working on".

I went across the road to wait for my turn. As I did not have much to do, I called Linda back home to check on her and work.

"Hello, darling; how are you?"

"OMG, Gaby; how are you? I thought you had disappeared in The Camino. Where are you and how are you?"

"I finished the Camino a few days ago; best thing I've ever done in my life. Now I am on my way to Fátima"

"Have you gone crazy? You've never been a religious person and now you have become a fulltime pilgrim?"

"No need to shout; I can hear you okay. And this pilgrimage is not about religion but about self-awareness, self-healing; it's about finding myself".

"Oh, dear, you sound different already. Where is the outrageous Gaby that left London not so long ago?"

"I left her somewhere along The Camino; it's been a long walk of self-discovery".

"How is everything in London?" I said trying to change the subject.

"Work is okay; the usual stress with clients and deadlines, but waiting for you, if you want your old job back".

"I'm not in a hurry".

We said good-bye and hung up. The call left me a bit shaken; I did not want to go back to that life; I had left the old Gaby somewhere in the Pyrenees.

Vivian came in the cafeteria a few minutes later. "Now is your turn".

I sat in front of Roberto in the lounge of his flat; he turned the fan on and closed the door to the balcony and the outside noise.

"What can I do for you?"

"I'm not quite sure, health wise I am fine but I've been struggling with my state of mind and the view I have of myself. I am usually very hard on me and my self-esteem is very low. I've been trying to find the solution on drinks, drugs, shopping, sex, Botox… and nothing worked; that's when I decided to take a sabbatical and I just finished walking The Camino".

"Mental issues are usually the most difficult to cure by a mainstream doctor and it would take you years of therapy with a psychiatry's that can guarantee the results, so, yes, this is something I can help you with. It's all about how we perceive ourselves. What we think and how we view ourselves is what we become, so I will help you shift that mental perception of yourself".

"And how are you going to manage that?"

"I will move the energy around you with acupuncture and work on your mental welfare".

He took me to another room and laid me down on a therapy table; he started putting needles all over me; I must have resembled a porcupine when he finished with me. He sat in a chair next to me and seized my wrist.

"Now close your eyes and bring to your forehead all the things that you don't like about yourself, really concentrate. Now, try to remember your childhood, your relationship with your parents and how they viewed you; this is very important because more often than not, what we think about ourselves in adulthood is brought from our childhood memories. Parents, siblings, school fiends sometimes can be very mean in what they say and those words can sometimes stay hidden deep down our memory and can cause lots of underlying mental problems. Just keep bringing to the surface all those issues that bother you and let me know when those images start fading away".

I am not sure how long I stayed lying there in that state of mind; I do remember crying a lot and then happy thoughts started popping in my mind and I started to smile. Roberto let go of the hold he had on my wrist.

"You can open your eyes now; I can see that your energy has shifted. I recommend you take things a bit easy during the next few days; no alcohol and try to rest as much as possible; sometimes you will feel low but most of the time you will begin to feel more elated and happier about yourself".

After taking all my needles out he gave me some homeopathic remedies and I went to meet Vivian.

"So, what did you think?"

"I'm not sure what he's done, but I've never felt this good about myself in ages", I said, beaming with joy.

"We need to find a place where we can have a few days' rest, maybe by the beach".

We asked the barman and he suggested a few places in the cost in the south of Galicia as we were heading to Portugal.

"There are a few beautiful beaches but if you need to relax and find a good place to stay, I suggest Playa de América in Pontevedra. Playa de Roda is also nearby, maybe more beautiful with white fine sand but there are no places to stay. You need to go to the bus terminal and get a bus to go there".

We found a nice hotel opposite the very long sandy beach; we just stayed there roasting ourselves under the sun, enjoying the magnificent view and the most amazing sunsets. We were both so tired we hardly even talked.

"I'm not sure what Roberto did to us but I have never felt so tired in my life".

"Don't worry, Gaby; it will only last until the body adjusts to all the energy changes that he did; it usually last around three days and then we can continue to Portugal. In any case, we needed a rest after walking the Camino".

"I am not complaining, but I didn't even feel this tired after walking 30 kilometres per day".

"You will see; in a couple of days you will feel the opposite; you will have so much energy that you will want to walk all the way to Fátima".

After three days of rest, we decided to start moving south. Our next stop, Porto, a coastal city in northwest Portugal known for its stately bridges and port wine. The first thing that hit me in Porto was the amount of noise and people, since it is a tourist hotspot. I was also totally in the hands of Vivian as being Brazilian she can speak Portuguese and although is similar to Spanish and I can speak Spanish, the Portuguese do not make any effort to understand the lingo; must be a historical issue with its neighbouring country. The old town had been built on the hills overlooking the Douro River, and its old streets are lined with cafes and bars; we went in one and I was dying for a well-deserved drink after three days of non-alcoholic rest.

"Two glasses of Port wine, please", Vivian asked the man behind the bar.

"Cheers!" I said toasting our wine glasses. "OMG this is too sweet; I can't drink this; is like drinking syrup; please can we have some Spanish Albariño?"

"We are in Portugal, please order a Portuguese wine, how about vino verde?" said the now quite angry bartender.

The vino verde was better but nowhere near as good as the Spanish wines. I had only been in Portugal for less than 24 hours and I was already missing Spain.

"I think Roberto didn't tune my energy to Portugal; I am feeling like a fish out of water here".

"Let's make a move and go to Fátima; the energy has to be better although there must be lots of tourists there too. Fátima is one of the most important catholic shrines and every year it attracts millions of pilgrims from all over the world".

We arrived to Fátima on an absolute scorching hot day, as I got down the bus, I noticed that from another bus that was parked next to ours a group of nuns all dressed in black was descending; one of them came running straight to me and started shouting while hitting me with a rosary.

"This is holy ground; you shouldn't be dressed like that; please show some respect". The other nuns came running to my rescue and restrained her but all gave me a disgusted look.

"God, Vivian, what was that all about; I am wearing shorts and a T-shirt, I am not exactly naked, but let's go to our hotel and cover ourselves up; I have been accused of many things in my life but being called "indecent" is a first".

The whole incident left me a bit shaken; when I got to the hotel I just wanted to stay there.

"Vivian, you go out on your own; I want to stay here and cool down; I need sometime on my own, please".

"Don't let an archaic religious mad Nun get the best of you".

"Is not just the Nun; I feel rundown. I need some time by myself".

"Okay, but I will be back tonight to take you to the main square", Vivian said as she went out.

As soon as she left, I started to cry. I looked at my mobile, not one message, not even one from George. Gaby, why are you doing this? There was not much wrong with your life: a good job, lots of young studs, why can't you be contented with just that?, why do you long for more? Maybe is time to forget all about this and go back to just being good old Gaby.

I must have dozed off. I was woken up that evening by Vivian.

"Come on, Gaby, wake up; we must go out now, you don't want to miss the light procession in the plaza".

We rushed out and as we approached the Cova de Iria, a huge plaza where a little chapel was built and where the Virgin Mary is believed to have appeared; I could see thousands of pilgrims already gathering there, all with a candle in their hands. A bishop led a procession of a statue of the Lady of the Rosary and soon we all started to pray. The sight of all the lit candles and the sound of the rosary being prayed by the thousands of people was very moving. I had goosebumps all over me and the energy was eerie. I then started to question myself again, was there more to life than a good job and a few possessions?; at least the thousands of people gathered here tonight clearly thought there was.

"The reason that you come to these places is to increase your energy levels. The power emanating from all these people gathered here tonight makes the energy even stronger and so if you rise your energy you will shine and help others shine too", Vivian said as if reading my mind.

"Why Fátima?"

"These is where the Virgin Mary appeared to three shepherd children; Lucia dos Santos and her two younger cousins, Francisco and Jacinta, and where the Virgin told them the three secrets and all the miracles that happened here. This is a sacred place and the energy has increased throughout the years of pilgrimage and prayer; you must have felt at least something here tonight".

"I did feel something; it's difficult to explain exactly what, but I am very overwhelmed by it all".

There are lots of places with high levels of energy around the world; most churches and temples are built on these places, hence the feeling of peace and calm when you go to them.

The following day we headed to Lisbon, where Vivian and I parted; she went back to Brazil and I took a flight to Málaga, where I was meeting with an old friend of mine from London. She had given up her life in wet and windy UK to retire in sunny Spain.

Málaga

Sophia was waiting for me at the airport, looking very refreshed and summery, she had long grey hair; a very slim woman, she was hardly wearing any makeup, yet she looked young and happy.

"Sophia, you are looking amazing; what on earth is your secret?"

"No stress, lots of sun and a glass of wine or two".

"I thought that lots of sun would give you lots of wrinkles".

"Misconception, sun is vitamin D: we need it for our hair and nails to grow, our skin to glow; nothing would grow or live without the sun. I am not saying that you should roast under the sun every single day but we should try and make the most of it and get some sun a few good hours every week. There are more illnesses that can develop though lack of sun that from too much of it".

"Well, that is sometimes difficult living in gloomy London".

"That's why I moved to Málaga; less stress and better weather".

We started driving along the coast towards Marbella, and stopped along the way in a lovely small restaurant by the sea. It was a small tavern with a few kiosks and a wonderful view of the sea.

"Buenos dias, señora Sophia, what can I get you today?" said a lovely waiter all dressed in white, wearing tennis shoes and as polite as only Spanish waiters are.

"Two glasses of house white, please, Pedro"

"You must come here often".

"Not as often as I would like to; the food here is delicious and very healthy. That is something that contributes to my wellbeing: good nutritious food, and not just swallowing it all down, but also taking the time to eat and enjoy it. Healthy food is our best medicine; we don't need drugs, we just need to eat what's right for our bodies. And what could be better than sitting down here with this wonderful view, a glass of good wine and a great friend to share it all with? Cheers", Sophia said, toasting our glasses of wine.

"So, how do you make a living, and how do you spend your days here in paradise?"

"My biggest income comes from renting my flat in Chelsea; the rents here are minimal compared to London and in general things are much cheaper. I give therapies from home and teach people how to eat well and live more meaningful lives".

"It looks as if I've come to the right place; that's exactly what I'm searching for, that's the reason why I left London and my lucrative job: I long for more. I feel like there is something missing; I can't really pinpoint it down to one item; I suppose it must be a series of things. You just made me realize that I don't pay much attention to food; I eat because I have to and anything that fills me up will do and I do gallop food down".

"Where do you normally eat?"

"I eat in front of the TV watching the news or anything that takes my mind away from whatever I'm eating", I said, a little bit fearful of what she might say.

"Have you ever read Eckhart Tolle's *The Power of Now?"*

"No, but I've heard of him; he has become very popular".

"It's no good hearing about things or knowing that something might be good for you. You have to try things for yourself; that is why we are here on this earth. We are spiritual beings having a life experience: to really feel things, to be happy, to be sad, to run, to dance, to actually do things that matter; unfortunately nowadays, people go in pursuit of material things and money, money, money, as if cash would fill that vacuum that you have right here", Sophia said while pushing me on my chest.

Pedro appeared with the two most spectacular goat cheese salads, served on a bed of kale, nuts and apple.

"That looks amazing", I said, complimenting my plate.

"I want you to really enjoy and taste every mouthful, taking your time, truly appreciating what you are putting into your body. This is the power of now, because "Now" is all there is".

It took us a long time to finish our lunch and I think this was the very first time I have actually savoured my food so much.

"Now, let's go to my flat, drop your rucksack and then I am going to take you shopping; I need to get you out of those clothes and drop the pilgrim look", Sophia said looking at me from head to toe.

"That sounds like a great idea; you are meant to go to Cape Finisterre after finishing The Camino in Santiago de Compostela and burn all your clothes there and so begin your new life but I never got round it".

"We can burn them here at the full moon beach party this Saturday".

"That's an even better idea, but not my hiking boots; they cost me a fortune".

Shopping in Spain is such a pleasant experience: shopkeepers are delightful and clothes are so much colourful and bright; back home they are usually black, grey or any dark colour.

"You also need a small suitcase; you can't keep travelling just with a rucksack".

"I don't know where I'm going next".

"A suitcase is a better place to keep clothes safe and tidy".

So it was that I left the shops with a new bag and a new wardrobe!

"And before we get back home, I must take you to the hairdresser", she said, and before I could say anything Sophia dropped me off at a saloon and asked the girl attending it to do a complete overhaul: "Haircut, blow dry, hands, feet and better check her legs for waxing; I don't want her to look hairy when she wears her new bikini.

"Call me when you are finished and I'll come and collect you".

It was late in the evening when I rang her up to come and collect me.

"Wow, Miss UK; you look ravishing. I love the new shorter haircut and not a grey hair in sight, we better go to a bar and have a drink to celebrate".

I was exhausted but agreed to go for a quick drink and some tapas.

"The way to a successful happy life is not just to work, eat and sleep but give yourself treats, pumper yourself and go out and enjoy it all. We do have to work for a living but make that job something you actually like; we spend most of the day working and if we don't enjoy it, it makes life pretty awful. And, most importantly, we have to find a balance and give ourselves time to enjoy all that hard work. Don't feel guilty about spending the money you have earned, save it for what? Remember there is only here and is NOW!"

"Thank you for such a wonderful indulging day, but right now all I can think about is going to bed".

I woke up the next morning and Sophia was in the balcony having breakfast overlooking the most magnificent view of the sea.

"So, this is what you wake up to every morning?"

"Morning, Gaby, come and join me. I prepared an oatmeal breakfast for both of us; you can improve it with berries, honey, nuts, cinnamon. Just add whatever you like. Having oats for breakfast is a good way to start your day as it's a gluten-free whole grain and a great source of important vitamins, minerals, fibre and antioxidants and it makes you feel fuller for a long period of time, stopping you from snacking".

"I usually just grab a coffee on my way to work; they know exactly what I like at my Costa coffee shop and I don't even have to open my mouth anymore, which makes my life much easier".

"Breakfast is the most important meal of the day; you shouldn't skip it but today the most important matter is that we are going to burn your old clothes, marking the beginning of a much healthier and meaningful life".

"Yes!!!"

"And I am going to introduce you to Manuel".

"Who is Manuel?"

"Manuel is my special friend, my lover, my one and only".

"Wow, if he is all that why on earth are you not living together?"

"Why do I want to spoil a perfect relationship with the monotony of marriage?; this way we get to share the best times and see each other when we want too; besides I like my own space and this way is just perfect for me. I won't be coming back here tonight so if you fancy someone, you are very welcome to bring him back here".

"I'm trying to avoid one-night stands but if I fall into temptation, I might do that. I want to do a bit of sightseeing so where do you recommend I go from here?"

"You are spoilt for choices around here; you can go to Marbella and Puerto Banús and see how the other half lives. There is a great street market there on Sundays so it would be a good place for you to go tomorrow; there is also Granada, with the grand examples of medieval architecture dating to the Moorish occupation, especially the Alhambra. You definitely have to go there! Seville is a bit further afield but it's a stunning place and you can always go and visit part of our country, Gibraltar, and take a ferry to Morocco, such a beautiful country. It's so close and yet you feel so far away; but, right now all we have to do is go to the beach".

That evening I took my old clothes to the beach party. Sophia announced that I had just finished walking the Camino and following the tradition, I was going to burn my old clothes and begin a new life. I then started burning my clothes in the bonfire amid a lot of cheering, loud music and dancing. It was quite surreal to be there surrounded by mostly young British expats cheering me up.

I danced until the early hours in the morning and truly felt that I had burnt my old me.

I woke up quite late but quickly took a bus to Puerto Banús, as I wanted to go to the street market that

Sophia had mentioned. I just followed the river of people as I stepped down from the bus, and soon the stalls of clothes lining the streets started to appear; the place was very crowded and it was quite hard to get close to the vendors. Soon enough the congestion and heat started to get the best of me as the hungover crept in. I decided to head for the marina, famous for having moorings for very large boats, including those of the King of Saudi Arabia and several of the world's wealthiest people. Its streets are lined with expensive luxury boutiques like Christian Dior, Gucci, Bulgari, Versace, Dolce & Gabbana. The marina was also very crowded, with tourists trying to spot any famous people in the boats and lots of attractive young women trying to get the attention of wealthy men. I soon realized that was not the place for me, so I took a taxi to nearby Marbella. What a contrast; the old town of Marbella's is a charming Spanish town with stoned streets, whitewashed facades: and what is not to like in a town where all its dustbins are hand painted by local artists? Why can't dustbins be turned into beautiful art pieces all over the world?; wouldn't this make earth a much nicer place to live?

I went into a small restaurant in the Plaza de los Naranjos and ordered a healthy tuna salad and a glass of my favourite Albariño. I remembered what Sophia said about enjoying the here and the now, and I relished every mouthful, and the view of all the tourist passing by; I was immersed in a world of my own. When I asked for the bill, the waiter said it had been paid for by a gentleman that had already left. I tried questioning him about the way he looked and why he didn't tell me earlier but could not get out much information from him.

I left looking everywhere; I thought I was being followed as I walked along the Avenida del Mar, which connects the old town with the beach, admiring the collection of ten sculptures by Salvador Dalí. I bought a chocolate and vanilla ice cream cone and went to the beach. I was thoroughly enjoying my cone but out of the corner of my eye, I could see a man gazing at me, like really staring. Eventually I stood up and walked towards him.

"Why are you staring at me?"

"Hello, my name is Richard; sorry to bother you but I really admire the way you enjoy your food" said a middle-aged man, with a bit of a belly and a kind face that put me at ease, as he didn't seem like a sociopath that was following me to eat me alive.

"So, you invited me for lunch?"

"Yes, but I didn't follow you here, I was already here when you arrived, making me jealous relishing your ice-cream. And I would love to eat one too but I'm trying to lose my belly", he said rubbing his stomach

"May I sit here?"

"Please do"

"Hello, my name is Gaby; where are you from?"

"I'm from Liverpool; you will only meet English people here in the Costa del Sol. Are you on holiday?"

"I'm staying with a friend in Málaga. I'm on a six-month sabbatical and just finished walking the Camino de Santiago and I'm here taking a break while I think were to go next".

"I own a villa near Fuengirola; I try and spend as much time as I can here in Spain; I love the laid-back attitude of Spanish life".

"What a coincidence; my friends flat is between Fuengirola and Málaga".

"Let me tell you; there are no coincidences in life, I am sure this was meant to be".

"I am not sure if it was meant to be but if you are going soon, I wouldn't mind a lift back home, I have a bit of a hungover and I am dreading having to wait for a bus".

"You were at the beach party last night, and it was your clothes we burnt in the bonfire?"

"Yep"

"You must be Sophia's friend; you see; there are no coincidences in life; this was meant to be; come on I'll take you home. No wonder you enjoy your food so much you must be following her guidance".

I just nodded and did not say a word. I was surprised as to how small the world sometimes seems to be.

Once in the car I started asking him about Sophia.

"How did you meet Sophia?"

"I am one of her patient's. I was very fat I used to eat food as an addiction just to fill in the gap that I was feeling within me; we start looking for love in all the wrong places and I was using food as a way to fill the void".

"I've just started to pay attention to food; for me it's always been a task that I needed to accomplish rather that something to cherish until Sophia pointed out to me".

"Well, you have really taken on board her advice. I thought you had always eaten with such gusto".

"It does make so much sense to enjoy food, as we have to do it all the time; I'm tuning into the power of now and relishing the momentum in everything that I do. I can't keep on rushing around life without paying attention to it I probably have been trying to block up that same void with other things but I do know what you mean as I do have that same feeling that something is missing from my life".

I was choking when I said that, as I realized there and then what a big void I had within me. We kept quiet after that and Richard came up to the flat when we arrived at Sophia's; she was there with Manuel and was very surprised to see us together when she opened the door.

And before she said anything, we said in unison:

"Serendipity!"

We sat in the balcony; I would miss that view when it was time to leave but for now, I just sat there with a glass of wine admiring the sunset. Richard offered to take me to the Alhambra in Granada early the following morning; then he left and I went to bed.

There were already many people queuing when we arrived and it was not even open but the view of the imposing red castle took my breath away.

"I have been here many times, but the imposing views of the Alhambra never ceases to amaze me", said Richard.

"I am very grateful for you taking your time to bring me here".

"The Alhambra dates from the 9th century and it was built by the Moorish, first as a military fortress and it wasn't until the 13th century that the royal residence was established and its lavish period began. And after the Moorish invasion ended, the Spanish royal family made lots of reforms and demolitions and the current church actually stands where the Mosque used to be; but Yusuf I and Mohammed V are responsible for most of the constructions of the Alhambra that we can still admire today".

"You are a good tourist guide, thanks for the information".

We walked through the gardens and into the impressive building and through the many patios including the Patio of the Lions. When we finished, we went to have lunch in a charming restaurant in the main square of Granada. The restaurant was advertising a Flamenco show that evening.

"If you want, we can find a hotel and we can come and see the show", said Richard

He must have seen the reaction in my face as he immediately said: "Don't worry, Gaby; we can get two rooms, I am not trying to take advantage of the situation, but I can't come to the show and then drive all the way back home. A few years ago, I would have jumped at the idea to get you in bed with me, but not now".

"A few months back I would have loved to; it was my addiction, the way to fill the void, but that's exactly what I am trying to change".

"As Louise Hay used to say "If you change your thinking you can change your life". Her book You can heal your life changed my life and once you start in the right track, the universe has a way of putting the right people in your path, the right book falls into your hands, a friend invites you to the right talk, you start meeting the right people, like us meeting yesterday and so forth. My life was spiralling out of control; too much food, meaningless relationships, and to top it up I was a workaholic; so I ended up in A&E with a heart attack and a friend of mine gave me that book as a present and it changed me completely. Best present ever".

"I was in a very similar situation and you are absolutely right; as soon as I started to think that maybe there was more to life and my soul started longing for more, I have met the right people, have done things that I have only dreamt of doing and for once I have gone with the flow and stopped giving excuses and building walls around me. So, let's book a table for the show here tonight and find a hotel. Let's go for it".

The show was amazing, so passionate and sexy, the dress so feminine and the man so masculine; God, it made me want to jump up and dance; we had lots of wine and a great time, made friends with everyone there and I realized that my life was heading in the right direction. But the following day I woke up with a big headache and I still had to wear the same clothes. Richard did not look much better either, and we both had to laugh. We had a coffee and headed home.

The next few days I spent mainly at the beach and having dinner with Sophia, Manuel and sometimes Richard. I thought about going to Seville but never got around it; in the end I decided to go to Morocco.

Richard contacted a tourist guide he knew in Tangier, that could drive me around the country and he also offered to take me to Gibraltar, to take the ferry from there. On the way there, he started to give me lectures and sounded just like my father.

"Morocco is not a safe place for a woman to travel by herself. And don't even trust Yousef, your driver: he will jump at any opportunity to hop into your bed. It's an Islamic country with deeply traditional culture and women are looked at in a different way as in the west and you should keep your shoulders and knees covered, especially if you are going to visit a mosque".

"Richard, I have travelled by myself many times, so don't worry".

"I do worry; I've grown very fond of you".

I did not reply. I could not even think about a relationship with anyone before I sorted out the relationship with myself.

As we arrived to Gibraltar all I could see was the famous Rock, but the place is so small that there are even traffic lights to let the planes land and take off, as there is not space for a runway away from it all. We went straight to the port and as I was going to say goodbye to Richard, he gave me a copy of Louise's Hay book *You can heal your life*.

"I hope this book helps you change your life the way it helped me change mine".

"I will treasure it".

"Don't treasure it, read it!"

As my ferry was not leaving for a few hours, I bought a coffee and started reading the book. I was so immersed in it I that nearly missed the announcement to board my ferry. The trip to Tangier crossing the Strait of Gibraltar takes only one hour and 30 minutes but I was glued to the view, as I get seasick quite easily.

Morocco

I arrived to the port and although it is so close to Spain it is like arriving at another planet. Men still wear tunics and women still cover their hair; after clearing customs I went outside trying to find my name amongst all the placards of the drivers waiting there; I went backwards and forwards and nothing, no "Gaby" written anywhere. One of the drivers saw me getting quite anxious and he helped me by calling the number that Richard gave me for Yousef, but he did not answer. I started walking to the information desk when I heard someone shouting my name. I raised my hand and he came straight at me all apologetic.

"Sorry, your ferry arrived at prayer time and I though you would take longer to come out, so I went to the place of worship".

I gave him "the look", handed over my bag and followed him to his car; this was not a good way to start my two weeks stay in Morocco.

Tangier is a port city with white washed facades and lots of hustle and bustle. Yousef drove me to the old town or as they call it, the Medina. We stopped in front of an old house.

"This is your riad for the night", said Yousef. Riads are boutique hotels in restored mansions, they are very affordable and very beautiful and Richard had said they were the best places to stay in Morocco. My room was stylishly decorated with authentic Moroccan furniture and the rooftop terrace was gorgeous, overlooking the town and the ocean in the distance. As it was quite late and I was very tired I requested to have something to eat there and then and I asked Yousef to come by the following day. Yousef insisted on staying with me until I went to bed and all I wanted was to be on my own; I just realized that since leaving London I had not slept or truly been alone and I missed that. Fortunately, the call for the sunset prayer started to sound from the mosque minaret's around Tangier.

"It's time for your prayer, go and pray and I'll see you here at 9am tomorrow". Finally and reluctantly he left. The melodious chanting of the call to prayer was captivating; I was somehow transported into another world. I closed my eyes and stayed in that faraway land until the waiter brought me back to earth with a tray of food.

"May I have a glass of wine please?"

"Sorry, Mam; this is a Muslim country we don't serve wine; only soft drinks or water".

"Sparkling, please". Two weeks without a drop of wine was going to be tough. I just wondered if the heavens were conspiring to get me sober and healthy.

I kept reading my book; Louise teaches how to live a positive and empowered life, with the aid of positive statements, which she called affirmations. Following her guidance, I stood in front of the mirror and started saying to myself: "I am beautiful, and everybody loves me". That proved somehow to be very difficult, but I kept repeating it, hoping that somehow I would start believing it.

The following morning, Yousef was waiting for me at reception. I took a good look at him now that I wasn't so angry for not showing up on time at the airport: he was quite handsome with olive skin, big black inquisitive eyes and a beautiful smile. We started walking along the alleyways filled with shops and teahouses The tourist touts were also plentiful but at least Yousef did a good job of shielding me from them. I loved the vibrant colours everywhere, the spices, the rugs and the smell of blossoms along the way. Yousef asked me not to buy anything in Tangier; he said as we were travelling south things would get cheaper.

"Have you ever had tagine?" asked Yousef. "A Tagine is an earthenware pot in which we cook our food; it's very healthy and delicious. There is a restaurant not far from here that belongs to a friend of mine; there we can go to the kitchen and they will show you how to cook a proper tagine".

We went around the backstreets until we found a very small restaurant. Yousef went to greet the owner and said a few things in Arabic to him. I was beginning to feel uneasy at not being able to understand what was said around me but the owner came towards me, greeted me very politely and asked me to follow him to the kitchen. I was expecting a catering style kitchen and instead it was just a room filled with lots of hot charcoal stoves and on top they would place the traditional tagine glazed pottery consisting of two parts: a circular base unit that is flat with low sides and a large dome-shaped cover that sits on the base during cooking. The cover is designed to return all condensation to the bottom and hence cook the food very much as a slow cooker probably does. The owner lifted a few tops and showed me different kind of tagine, lamb, fish, vegetable and chicken; they all smelled delicious. He showed me all the species and explained how each dish has its special mixture of them. I chose a chicken and a vegetable tagine and asked him to show me to the toilet. I went into the ladies and all I could see was a hole in the ground. OMG, no toilet! I had to crouch and hold my breath. This was definitely another planet. I went to the table and there the two tagines were waiting for me together with a basket of flat bread.

"May I have a knife and fork please?"

"Sorry, we don't use knives and forks in Morocco; we use our hand and bread to eat our food, we wash our hands afterwards but I can ask if they have some cutlery".

"Don't worry; I'll give it a try".

I just looked at Yousef and copied what he did; however, he managed to put everything in his mouth and half of mine landed on the table. The food was delicious and I savoured every mouthful. Sophia would have been proud of me.

In the afternoon, we went to the Kasbah located high on a hill in Tangier, with fantastic views of the ocean. The old Sultan's palace lies within the Kasbah's walls. It is known as Dar El Makhzen and is now a museum of Moroccan art. At the end of the day, I was tired after the days walking and sightseeing so I asked Yousef to leave me at my riad; I wanted an early night, specially as we were going to leave early in the morning toward Chefchaouen. I went to the roof terrace again and sat there looking at the horizon; this was the time of the day when I really missed that glass of wine, so I closed my eyes and dreamt of one. A feeling of peace engulfed me when I let go of all the worries of the day; I could hear the subtle chanting of the call for prayer, I entered into a state of peace within me that I had not been able to achieve before. I am not sure how long I stayed in this state but when I opened my eyes, the sky was turning darker and the stars were beginning to twinkle.

The following day we headed for the blue city, Chefchaouen; as we approached it, I thought we were getting close to heaven; the entire city is painted in light blue and it feels like you are arriving to bliss. We had to leave the car in the outskirts of the city as no cars are allowed in the centre of town and we had to walk through the narrow streets to my next riad. We were pestered by men offering hashish: the Chefchaouen region is one of the main producers of cannabis in Morocco and apparently tourist go there for that very same reason so I imagined that between the cannabis and the blue painted walls of the city you must feel like in paradise. My room had a big balcony overlooking the mountains as Chefchaouen is surrounded by them and the cool breeze made it less hot and humid than Tangier. After a while, I ventured out of the streets on my own and within minutes, I was surrounded by touts offering cannabis and I bought a spliff. I went back into my room and sat in the balcony and had a few puffs. If I couldn't have a glass of wine, at least I could enjoy getting high. I did not really feel much or at least I did not notice anything, at that moment. Yousef came by and asked me if I wanted to go out to eat something.

"I would love to eat something; I am a bit peckish", I said with a bit of a giggle

We found a small petite restaurant and Yousef ordered the food. I asked for a large bottle of water, as I was getting very thirsty.

The food arrived and it smelt and looked delicious. I was getting better at eating with my hands and I enjoyed it so much and just could not stop it.

"You have a bit of an appetite today", he said looking at the way I was eating everything. Or maybe I was not leaving much to eat for himself.

"You can order more if you want to; I feel I can eat an elephant today", I said giggling even more.

As we went out of the restaurant, I was giggling even more and Yousef gave me an inquisitive look.

"Have you smoked anything?"

"I went out and bought a joint earlier on and had a few puffs but I didn't feel a thing; I must have bought the wrong stuff", I said laughing out loud.

"I am sure you bought the right stuff; you are acting really weird. I better take you back to your riad and you better sleep it over".

As he said that, I felt a bit dizzy and I struggled to walk back to the riad through the narrow steep lanes of Chefchaouen. Yousef helped me up to my room and for a minute there I thought he was trying to take advantage of the situation and stay there with me, but Richard's words popped into my head and I quickly ushered him out of my room. The following day I woke up with a big headache. I picked up was what left of the joint and chucked it down the toilet.

"From now on it's just going to be water, Gaby", I said it as I watched the joint disappearing down the drains.

Yousef came by and asked me if I was feeling okay or if I wanted to spend the day resting.

"I am okay now and will feel even better after I have some breakfast".

"You better don't smoke anymore because with that appetite you won't fit into my car by the end of your trip", he said smiling.

"Don't worry; I already got rid of what I had left and if I ever see another man trying to sell me anymore, I will chase him myself down the road with a hammer in my hand".

Yousef laughed out load. "That happens to all the tourist that come here; they think the cannabis hasn't affected them and when they least expected it kicks in. At least I was there to take you back to bed; most of the time you see them sleeping it off on the streets as they can't find their way back to their hotels".

"But the food tasted so delicious and I just wanted to eat and eat; I must have put on ten kilos. I better eat lettuce all day today".

"I still don't understand why you always have to try and find something to make you feel good, either with alcohol or drugs. All you need is to feel good about yourself, good company, good food, good music but to try and get high or drunk to spoil it all is beyond me".

Yousef was right, why on earth when we were having a good time, we had to spoil it all by getting blasted and maybe forgetting all about the good time we were having, not to mention the hungover.

We walked in silence for a while.

"Where are we going today?"

"Today we are going to visit the Kef Toghobeit Cave. It's the deepest cave in Morocco and it's not far from here and then we can stroll around the city; it's a good place for shopping if you want to buy something, I can show you a few shops".

"That all sound great but let's start with shopping. I've seen lots of silver jewellery and would like to buy something nice".

"Better the cave first and then we will have all the afternoon to just take it easier around town; tomorrow we are going to Fez, which is a World Heritage Site and there is lots to see there, so better take it easy today.

We drove through the mountains to reach the cave along a beautiful scenery. When we reached the cave we were given helmets and the guard asked us to stay very close to each other and not to wonder on our own. We were going down and down through very narrow passages; I was beginning to feel very claustrophobic and hot and sweaty; I was about to ask Yousef if we could get back up again when we reached an opening in the cave and to my relief our guide said that this was as far as we were going to go. When he said that, he turned all the lights and the torches off and everything went pitch black and when I say black, I mean black; I put my hand right in front of my nose and I could not see it. Another tourist screamed and begged the guide to turn the lights on; we gave a sigh of relief and quickly turned around and started climbing back to the surface. When I reached the entrance to the cave and put a step out of it and I felt the warmth of the sun and felt the breeze on my face I realized that was all I needed to feel good. I had everything to make me happy right in front of me and yet I was always searching for more. But shopping was always good and I had my eyes on some earrings I had seen while walking earlier on.

On the way to Fez we stopped in Volubilis, an old Roman city considered the ancient capital of the kingdom. It is very well preserved and I have always been interested in ancient buildings, and how they take us back in history. It reminded me that even then people were not happy with what they had; the Romans were always searching to extend their empire and in the end it was their downfall. I think we have to be more grateful with what we have and appreciate it a bit more. Maybe that search could lead us to our own defeat.

As we approached Fez, I was taken aback to see how large it was, but the closer we got the more beautiful it looked. The medina is surrounded with fortified walls with watchtowers and scattered gates along the walls, each one more breathtakingly beautiful than the other.

"The riad you are staying tonight it's the most luxurious of all the riads where you'll be staying in Morocco; it has a traditional Hammam and spa with massage treatments. You should try the oriental massage when you get there and maybe eat at the restaurant; there is also wine in this riad as it is run by a Spanish company. I am staying with friends tonight and I'd like to spend some time with them if you don't mind, but I will come and pick you up early so we can start the tour of this great city".

"Don't worry you go and have a good time with your friends; I'm going to book that massage straight away; it sounds amazing and this riad looks wonderful so I am sure I will have a good evening on my own".

My bedroom was grand with a four-poster bed and very tastefully decorated. I could have just stayed there but I went to the massage room to have the oriental massage, which included the use of different oils, aromatherapy and soft music. It was very relaxing and I soon fell asleep. I'm not sure for how long, but when I woke up the therapist had left and I just went to the bar and ordered a glass of white wine. However, it didn't taste as good as I had dreamt it. Or maybe I was beginning to change my sensitivity and a glass of water wasn't that bad after all: it was free and good for you and in fact up to 60% of the human adult body is water. Thank God it's not made of wine….

Fez lived up to the expectations: an outstanding medieval town that up to this date is still the largest car-free urban area, with only donkeys used as means of transport. The alleyways are filled with shops and there are lots of hidden architectural gems as well as mosques all over the place. After three days of touring the city during the day and enjoying the spa during the evenings, it was time to move on.

"Yousef, is there a quieter place we can go to now? I need a bit of peace and quiet after all the hustle and buzzle of Fez".

"We can go to the desert; there is no quieter place on earth than the desert. It's quite a long drive between the Atlas Mountains but a very beautiful one, maybe we can stop one night along the way to take a rest".

"That sounds amazing; I've been dreaming of going to the desert since I saw the film Laurence of Arabia".

"Good, we can drive to Erfoud; that's where my family is from; we can probably stay at my parents' home: my mother is always pleased to see the tourist I am driving around Morocco. Erfoud is very close to the Sahara. I am sure you will love the desert; it's the only place on earth where you can hear your heart beat. It's so quiet".

"I don't know about staying at your parents' house; I rather stay in a riad".

"My family will feel offended if we don't stay with them. My mum will love to teach you how to cook a proper tagine".

"Are you sure they won't mind?"

"They will love to have you there, I promise. I will phone my mum straight away". After a while of him talking in Arabic and what I thought was a heated discussion, Yousef asked me: "What kind of tagine you want for dinner?"

"Chicken".

And after that, we set towards the dessert; the Sahara was waiting for me, I was really looking forward to that.

After seven hours driving, we arrived at Yousef's parents' house; I was pleasantly surprised: it was a modern town house and very clean. The family welcomed me as if I was a family member they had not seen in ages and his mother, Fatima, took me to my bedroom, which was upstairs next to the terrace with lovely views of the town. Only the father spoke any English and I do not speak Arabic nor French, the two main languages in Morocco so I was at the mercy of Yousef translating for me. He came behind his mother and asked me if I wanted to take a rest and showed me the bathroom.

"Come downstairs when you want to; mother will be waiting in the kitchen for you".

I gave her a big smile and thanked her. I went to the bathroom and the toilet was the traditional hole in the ground, "Oh, Dear Gaby, breath Ommmmmm". I took a shower, went to the terrace and did my evening meditation; it was getting to be a good way to calm down and I was adding it to my daily routine. I was discovering that quieting my mind for a short while would give me that peace I had been craving for; it was not always simple to quiet the mind but it was getting easier every day. There was a short mention in Louise Hay's book and she said that the best way to calm your mind was concentrating on the breathing and it worked. I was swapping my usual glass of white wine for meditation and it was beginning to pay dividends; I was feeling much better with myself, more relaxed and things started to bother me a lot less. And I was also learning to flow with the situations that life was throwing at me.

I went down to the kitchen and Fátima was waiting for me; the kitchen wasn't the modern fitted kitchen I had back home but it was very welcoming; there was a big table in the centre of the room and all the women were sitting around it preparing something for the meal we were about to cook. I could see that this was a female only territory and that not even Yousef was welcomed there. There were two younger sisters and the wife of the eldest brother; she could mumble a few words in English.

"Seat, seat, me show you".

They were all wearing traditional long Islamic clothing and headscarves and although I was wearing a not too short dress with sleeves, I felt a bit bare.

Fátima, as if reading my mind, wrapped her arms around me and tried to tell me that I was okay. She shouted something to Yousef and he came running to let me know that they did not expect me to wear a headscarf, as I was a westerner. Fátima grabbed my hands and started showing me all the herbs and species and how to prepare the tagine; once we left it in the stove, she showed me how to cook the couscous; the sisters were preparing the dough for the bread; they all worked together chatting and smiling to each other. I wondered what they were talking about and how different their lives were compared to mine; theirs revolved around that kitchen table; mine around the board meeting table at work.

The following morning the whole family woke up to say goodbye. Fátima was crying and all the drama shook me a bit; I had never ever seen my mother cry when we parted and yet this woman that I barely knew, that I hadn't even been able to communicate with words was sad because I was leaving. This really moved me and I also had a lump in my throat.

We arrived quite early at a hotel by the edge of the Sahara. I could see the dunes and the vast bareness of the landscape; it looked wonderful. Yousef went to try to sort out a caravan of camels that would take us to spend the night somewhere inside the dessert, so I started to walk in the sand. I stood in one of the dunes and stayed there watching a few falcons circling the skies, searching for pray but all I could see was sand and more sand.

Yousef came and joined me.

"It's wonderful; wait until you spend the night in the middle of that vastness; you will love it. We are all set there; is only a couple of Americans travelling with us tonight, we will leave around 5pm when the sun starts to go down and the temperature drops, so you can spend the day in the hotel's swimming pool if you want".

There were a few people by the swimming pool; most had spent the previous evening in the desert and they were all talking about it and how surreal it had seemed. I could not wait to get out there. I read and slept a bit during the day until it was time to leave.

Yousef came by to pick me up around 4pm and said I should only wear loose clothes, as there would not be a place to change into pyjamas and a proper toilet facility.

As I came out of the hotel all the camels were waiting outside; the men were wearing long cotton robes and turbans, even Yousef; I just thought I was stepping into a film set. The American couple came out wearing matching khaki safari outfits.

Getting up on the camels proved to be quite difficult, but once I was comfortable seating on it, Yousef started pulling mine and slowly one by one the camels started moving, forming quite a long caravan heading towards the desert. Around an hour into our journey, we came into a halt and we all got down and sat on the edge of the dunes to watch the sunset; if you think that the sunset by the sea is the best ever, that's only because you haven't been to the desert and watch one. We reassumed our journey and we kept on going for another hour or so until we reached a small oasis; we all got down and the camels went on to drink water and the men set camp, making a fire and erecting tents around it.

After dinner, Yousef sat next to me and handed me a blanket.

"Como on, let's walk to the top of a dune; better bring a blanket because it does get very cold at night in the desert".

It was hard walking up the hill in the sand; my feet just kept going under and very little progress was made, but Yousef showed me how to walk sideways and we eventually got to the top of the hill. The sight of the sky was breath taking. It felt as if I could nearly touch the Milky Way, the shooting stars seemed in slow motion and I could swear they were falling just nearby. Yousef put his arm round my waist and held me tight next to him. My body started to shake; I could feel where this was heading, but the thought of making love under that beautiful sky in the middle of the desert with a Bedouin was way too much temptation and I just couldn't resist it. He started to undress me and caress my body in a way that transported me into a world of passion and extreme pleasure. I could just make up the silhouette of his muscular body under the shadow of a crescent moon, but my God!, he was a stunning man. I was transported into the Arabian nights of my childhood dreams and completely let go of all my inhibitions. We stayed there in a passionate embrace not saying anything and the only thing that I could hear was the sound of my heart beating. I was woken up by the first sight of the sun rising between the dunes; I could have just stayed there looking at the horizon, but Yousef jumped up and pulled me out of my trance.

"We have to leave quickly before the sun rises and it starts to get hot".

We got back to the camp and everyone was already up and getting ready to leave. And before I knew it, I was back in the camel and heading back to the hotel. The journey back was much faster and nobody spoke; when we arrived, I went to my room and fell asleep for a few hours; later on when I woke up, I went to the swimming pool. The American woman was there by herself and I took a sunbed next to her.

"Hi, how are you today? Did you have a nice rest?"

"Yes, thank you; and you?"

"I couldn't sleep much; my husband is snoring too loud so I came out here to have a rest. And you? I didn't see much of you last night; you disappeared with that handsome young man".

"Please, don't remind me; I am already starting to regret it".

"Why regret it, I wished I had spent the night making love with a gorgeous man in the middle of the Sahara. What a beautiful memory to treasure. Just imagine when you are old and you look back in life and you remember this one night. I am sure it will bring you a big smile and a look in your face that will leave everyone guessing what you were fantasising about".

"My friend that recommended him as a tour guide warned me about it".

"So what? He didn't tell you your tour guide was so strikingly beautiful and don't you ever regret what you did; just regret what you didn't have the courage to do; opportunities don't come back in life, so only regret what you missed".

"I did have a fab night, but what do I do the rest of the trip?"

"Do what you heart tells you is right and don't look back; you are not going to marry him. Just enjoy it while it lasts"

At that moment, her husband turned up.

"Hi, girls; having a good time here in the sun?"

His wife just gave him "the look", at which point I left as I could just feel an argument just starting to brew about someone snoring too loud.

I went to my room and a few minutes later there was a knock on my door; it was Yousef: "Would you like to go out to dinner?"

"I'm starving; give me five minutes I'll meet you at reception".

Yousef took me to a very quaint restaurant; we sat in the terrace that had a wonderful view of the desert.

We were both very quiet and hardly looked at each other, but it was Yousef that broke the silence.

"I'm sorry about last night; your friend Richard asked me not to seduce you, but I could not stop myself last night, I am sorry".

"Why sorry? Do you regret what happened?"

"Regret no, it was absolutely magical, and it was not the usual tourist seduction; it was very special for me".

"So, why make a big issue about it?; we both had a great time last night, better keep that beautiful memory in our hearts and enjoy the rest of my time here in Morocco. Where are we going from here?"

"Marrakech, the most enchanting city in the world. You will love it there, but it would take us a couple of days, maybe three depending if you want to stay in some of the places along the way".

It took us three days to reach Marrakech as we decided to visit the Ouzoud Waterfalls, the second highest in Africa. Yousef resumed his duties as a tourist guide, never trying to seduce me again. I was happy about it as I did not have to choose and I would always treasure what happened in the desert as something magical.

My stay in Morocco mas coming to an end and I still did not know what to do next; I could go back to Spain or travel somewhere else but did not know where. I called Sophia to see if she had any suggestions.

"Hello, darling, how is Morocco treating you?"

"Morocco had been absolutely marvellous, but I am not sure where to go next, I thought you could help me point in the right direction".

"Well, you are very welcome back here; but as it's your sabbatical. Why not try somethings as exotic as India; you could stay in the Ashram I went to and maybe you can find that hero inside yourself that you are searching for".

"India sounds absolutely great; please send me an email with all the details of the Ashram and anything you can think of that would be good for me to visit".

"Will do, and look after yourself".

I was excited about going to India, and I asked Yousef to take me to a travel agency.

"There are no direct flights to Delhi and the cheapest would be via Istanbul; why don't you stay there a few days? It's a fantastic city and a good way to break such a long journey", said the travel advisor

"Istanbul sounds great; I always wanted to go there, as it's the only city located in two continents"

"When do you want to leave?"

"The day after tomorrow".

Yousef, who was sitting next to me, jumped

"Can you stay at least another day; I wanted to take you to Essaouira, a port city an hours' drive from here and tomorrow night is the jazz festival; it is quite something".

"I can't say no to a jazz festival and better have an extra day to recover; so, three more days in Morocco, then a week in Istanbul and on to Delhi and then, who knows?"

Yousef looked happy; he held my hand as we left the travel agency and walked around the traditional souks. I was glad he was there to shield me from the nuisance of the tourist touts. Marrakech, also called the red city, is really magical; especially the Jama El f'na Market, although I hated all the cobra snakes appearing from inside the baskets. We passed La Mamounia hotel, a 7-star hotel where a stay could probably cost me my entire budget for my sabbatical, so I just looked at it from a distance.

Essaouira is a vibrant port surrounded by walls, a mixture between French, Spanish and African cultures. The jazz festival was going to take place in the main square near the port; there were many people already walking around the town when we arrived. Yousef took me to my riad, so I could drop my bags; my bedroom had an impressive four-poster bed and a balcony with a view to the sea. I wondered if he had something in mind when he had chosen it; after all I was going to spend my last two nights in Morocco, why worry about it now, when I had a jazz festival to attend.

The first band was already playing when we arrived at the venue, and most people were dancing; we also joined in and I just let go and enjoyed the moment. I was truly happy; the energy of the people, the music and being just there enjoying the occasion not thinking of anything else, past or future it's what makes special moments in life so amazing. Yousef looked also very happy; he was wearing very tight black jeans and a white shirt that enhanced his beautiful smile, the buttons were opened half way through. I just gave a sight and thought of the four-poster bed. When we arrived. I held his hand tight and would not let go; he came to my room and started kissing me.

"I've dreams of this since the dessert".

"So why didn't you?"

"I was waiting for you to invite me to your room; you are not like any other tourist, you are special".

After that, we did not say anything else; we just got lost in that huge four-poster bed....

We spent all day in the bedroom only venturing out the following evening to stroll around the narrow streets of Essaouira and to eat my last tagine. The following day we drove back to Marrakech so I could catch my flight to Istanbul. It was hard to say goodbye; at the airport I had a lump in my throat and so did he.

"I'll be waiting for you to come back to me; you can stay here with me forever".

I looked at him and quickly left; I knew that it would probably be the last time I ever saw him, as I could not envision myself leaving the last of my days around that kitchen table in Erfoud.

Istanbul

As I was walking down the plane aisle towards my seat, I heard someone calling my name

"Gaby, Gaby". I could not believe my bad luck; it was the American couple from the desert. I did not want to see anyone, especially not those that had witnessed my affair with Yousef; and worst of all, my seat allocation was taking me closer and closer to them. I ended up sitting in the row just behind them.

"Fancy meeting you here, on this flight to Istanbul".

"What a coincidence", I said with a very surprised look on my face.

"There are no coincidences in life, my dear".

Oh no, those were exactly the same words Richard told me when we met, so better change the negative way I am thinking about this and turn it into something positive. I sat down on the window seat and just kept looking to the horizon. Maybe it was not such a bad thing meeting these two; at least it had taken my mind of Yousef. The two seats next to me remained empty and after the take-off, I was ready to stretch when the American lady sat next to me.

"I hope you don't mind me seating here, you can tell me what happened with your gorgeous tourist guide during the rest of the trip?"

"I am so sorry to ask but I am terrible with names and I can't remember neither yours or your husbands?" I said lowering my head in an apologetic manner.

"I'm Jill and my husband the snorer is Peter. So, tell me what happened?"

"Nothing much happened after that night", I said not wanting to tell her anything of my last two days in Essaouira.

"But I saw you at the airport giving him a passionate kiss".

"I wouldn't call it passionate; it was just a kiss".

"Will leave at that, so what made you come to Istanbul?; last time I saw you didn't have a clue of where you were going next".

"I'm actually on my way to India and Istanbul just happened to be a stopover, so I decided to stay for a few days to break the journey. And you, why are you travelling to Istanbul, I thought you were going back to America?"

"My husband has been diagnosed with terminal cancer and he doesn't have long to live; so, before he gets too ill to travel, we decided to go and visit all those places we had in our bucket list. That's why I said to you don't ever regret what you did, but regret instead the things you didn't do. I do regret lots of things we put off because of one stupid thing or another and now we have to rush and do things that we always wanted to do but now we find it difficult to enjoy due to the circumstances".

"I am so sorry to hear that, I would never have guessed; he looks fit and I've never heard him moaning".

"I'm the moaner"; I even complain about his snoring as he asked me not to treat him any different and I am sure that when he is gone, that is what I am going to miss the most".

I held her hand and did not say anything else; I could see she was crying and really hurting inside.

We landed in Istanbul and into a big chaos. I was really glad I had not landed there on my own. What a mess! We stayed very close together as we queued for hours before we cleared immigration but finding our bags was even more chaotic and finally we managed to jump into a taxi. We gave the taxi driver both of our hotel addresses and he just gave us a big smile. When we arrived, the hotels were literally across the road from one another; we looked at each other and we all said in unison: "There are no coincidences in life". And we burst out laughing

The next few days we spent touring around that magnificent city; it must be one of the most fabulous in the world. The feeling of grandeur starts just standing in front of the two great Mosques; Hagia Sophia and The Blue Mosque. We visited the Topkapı Palace, the home of the Ottoman Sultans for a long time, with stunning views of the Bosporus river. When we walked past the room where the sultan's harem was kept I wondered if in a past life I might have lived there waiting every night to be chosen as his favourite concubine and thought that I could have worn all the fabulous jewellery kept in the palace museum. I laughed at myself when I walked in front of a mirror, wearing no makeup, no jewellery, a pair of shorts and trainers, not the sight of a Turkish Goddess, but then, there is nothing wrong with dreaming.

The most amazing time we spent was in the Grand Bazar, one of the largest and oldest covered markets in the world. As I started haggling with stall tender for the price of a scarf, Peter quickly stepped in and paid the full asking price. I looked at him and said: "You didn't have too, and I am sure you could have paid half the amount you paid him".

"I know I could have paid less than half the amount I paid, but I can afford the full price and the people you haggle with in these markets have large families to feed, so if I pay them the full price weather is fair or not, I know I am helping them. You can call it charity, but to me, it just helps me sleep better".

"I've never thought about it in that way".

"We were in a market in Machu Picchu in Peru a few years ago, and I was trying to pay as little as possible for an alpaca wool hat and after I paid for it, the poor Indigenous woman started to cry and thanked me because she was going to be able to feed her family with the little money I paid her, as she had not been able to sell anything else that day. I realized there and then how much they depend on the tourist and how unfair the whole issue of haggling really is; there I was travelling in full luxurious comfort paying a fortune for the whole trip and yet when I had to buy from someone that really needed the money, I felt elated to pay very little for their precious products. I immediately apologized to her and gave her all the money I had left; I had a lump in my throat and I vowed never to haggle again on a street market".

"What a beautiful story, it has really touched me and I would never haggle again. You are so right Peter, those few pennies I was saving would probably do a lot better in someone else's pocket than in mine".

I left the market being the proud owner of a full priced scarf and that afternoon we sailed in a boat along the Bosporus river, admiring the city that lies between two continents: to the north of the river Europe and to the south Asia. So much history, such imposing beauty. I still had the feeling I had once lived there and it was not my first time sailing along those waters. I felt a bit nostalgic as if there was more hiding from me in this city.

That evening we went to a see a Sufi dance or whirling dervish, a type of meditation inspired by the Persian poet Rumi, whom was believed to whirl up to three days and nights. It is performed only by men and is a traditional form of Sufi worship, a continuous twirling with one hand pointed upward reaching for the divine and the other hand pointed toward the ground. They were all dressed in white with brown elongated hats. Just watching and listening to the music transported me to another world I closed my eyes and once again I had that feeling of déjá vu and I started to cry. Jill noticed I was crying and she looked at me with an inquisitive expression.

"Why are you crying? Are you missing your handsome Moroccan guy?"

"No, nothing like that. He hasn't even crossed my mind, but since I landed in Istanbul I've been having this strange feeling as if I've lived here before and tonight with these dancers and music I was transported to a memory that is there but I can't really reach... As if this is not the first time I have ever set foot here in Turkey".

"And you've never been here before?"

"Not in this life time, this is my very first time here".

Peter that was listening to our conversation quickly intervened.

"I've been reading a book, *Many Lives, Many Masters*, by Dr Brian Weiss, the true story of a psychiatrist, his young patient and the past-life therapy that changed both their lives. I've nearly finished it: perhaps you would like to read it and help you out with this feeling you are having, maybe you have lived here before and being in the place has prompted you to remember that life"

"The first time I had this feeling was back in the Topkapı Palace harem's room, so maybe I was really a favourite concubine of one of the sultans. That would have been great".

Both Jill and Peter burst out laughing

"Trust you to think you were a concubine", said Jill still laughing out loud.

"I'll have to look more into this; please Peter finish the book before we go our own separate ways as I don't think I can buy books in English here in Turkey and I would love to ready it and find out a bit more about past lives and how they influence my behaviour in this one. Having been a concubine in a past life could explain a lot of my behaviour in this one..."

"I think Peter must have been a sultan, he behaves like one most of the time".

We went walking along the streets of Istanbul, all jockeying about who we could have been in a past life, but the concubine was still my number one option. But soon after, our relaxed enjoyable evening came to an abrupt end when we heard a loud bang and everything went dead quiet for a minute or so. After a little while we heard lots of people screaming and running; police started appearing everywhere, I could hear lots of sirens and helicopters hovering in the skies. Peter held both Jill's and my hands.

"A bomb has exploded; quick we have to start running but don't let go". We ran towards a main road, trying to find a taxi to take us back to the hotel but the whole place was in total chaos, a tourist double decker bus was parked on the road and the bus driver ushered us in. We jumped in the bus and as soon as it was full the driver quickly left. I peeped out the window and it looked like Armageddon; my heart was pounding so fast I thought I might just have a heart attack. I looked at Jill and she was holding tight to Peter, she just looked at me and said: "That is why you have to live your life to the fullest and regret nothing; only what you didn't have the guts to do".

We went to Jill's and Peter's hotel and straight to the bar.

Peter ordered a bottle of champagne.

"We have to celebrate life".

The toast was very emotional after what we had just been through and Peter´s condition. I was still shaken and when the barman turned the TV on, we could see how close we had been to the actual explosion; the bomb had been detonated by a suicide bomber. We wondered if he had walked past next to us, or what would have happened if we had walked faster. We learned that there had been some casualties amongst them a few tourists. We were drinking champagne but it was difficult to feel cheerful.

I went back to my hotel and turned my mobile on. OMG, it just started bleeping and bleeping; I must have had at least a hundred messages from all my friends and family, all wanting to know if I was okay. If only they knew how close I had been to the blast they would probably beg me to cut my sabbatical short, but I had no intention of giving up yet. I kept hearing Jill's words in my head, "Only regret what you didn't have the guts to do!" so I just wrote back telling everyone I was safe in my hotel.

The next day was our last day in Istanbul and after the previous evening´s event, we decided to spend the day sunbathing by the pool and just chill out; we didn't feel safe going around the city anymore. I took Louis Hay's book; I wanted to try to finish it as I intended to give it to Peter as I thought it could really help him.

Jill was already by the pool; she looked like a fifty's movie star, wearing a large hat and glasses and very red lipstick.

"Morning Jill, did you manage to get some sleep?"

"After all the champagne we drank last night "The Sultan" was in his very best snoring form, so not a very good night sleep for me. How about you?"

"It took me a while to reply to all my messages and to calm down but had a good sleep in the end".

"Gaby, now that we are friends and we have all day long, are you going to tell me what really happened with Yousef?"

"Oh no, I've just been hit by another bomb! All I can say is that I did follow your instructions and I've got nothing to regret".

"That is not good enough; come sit right next to me and tell me all the juicy bits".

There was no place to escape to, so I did sit and told her all about our two days in Essaouira.

"Are you planning on going back?"

"No, that would spoil the memory of those magical days".

"When Peter is gone, he made me promise I would have a have a boob's job and live the rest of my life to the fullest he even suggested I should go visit you in London so I could take advantage of your personal male harem there".

"Do you even talk about what would happen afterwards?"

"The cycle of life and death is a natural incidence and life itself is a privilege; so why waste it dwelling on what we can't change. We have to make the most of it and enjoy life. I am sure Peter and I will meet again in the afterlife and maybe share another life together but we believe that the time I have to remain here on earth in this lifetime, I should not waste it crying".

"And talking of the devil, here comes your sultan".

"Morning, girls, enjoying yourselves talking about me?"

"It's nearly afternoon and we weren't exactly talking about you, but about Gaby's harem and how I should go and visit her".

"At least wait until I am gone", he said blinking an eye at Jill and handing me his book. "When you read this, you'll know will meet again, and that probably we have shared a few lives together. I've had that feeling I have known you before since the first time we met; only that in the desert you were too busy to take any notice of us".

I went bright red and searched for my book *You can heal your life* and handed it to him. "

Maybe we can meet again in this lifetime.....you can try and heal your life and enjoy this one a bit longer".

I gave him a big hug and started to cry. "No crying, please, Gaby".

"I am only crying because tomorrow we are going our separate ways and it's been a great privilege to share this time here in Istanbul with you guys. Bomb and all it's been amazing".

Peter ordered more champagne and this time we really enjoyed every minute that we had left together.

India

Taking off from Istanbul was harder than I ever thought it would be; it was supposed to have been just a stop over and it had turned out to be much more than that. It had taught me many things and I would never underestimate the importance of making the most of every second in our lives; you never know what it's coming round the corner, I could have died in that explosion. I thought of Peter trying to make the most of what little life he had left, but for now I was heading to India.

Arriving in Delhi was even more chaotic than landing in Istanbul and I was on my own. It was very late at night as the plane had been delayed in Istanbul. After a long time queuing in immigration, I was told I was in the wrong counter and I had to start all over again. I saw a couple of very tall American guys and I asked them for help but they were not exactly as friendly as I was hoping for. At least I felt a bit safer standing next to them.

When I finally manged to get into a taxi and gave the driver the name and address of the hotel; he looked a bit horrified and asked me:

"Are you sure you want to go there, Mam?"

"Yes, please".

"Mmmmmm".

I wondered what was that all about; after all this was the hotel that Sophia had recommended. She had said it was in a very good location that would give me a good flavour of Indian life. It was very late at night so I couldn't see much of Delhi; we passed a few temples and lots of tuck-tucks everywhere. We arrived at a very noisy and bumpy road; I could see cows and rubbish on the street and there in the middle of it all I saw the sign of my hotel, Hari Park Hotel. OMG I was going to faint; the first thing that crossed my mind was that I was going to strangle Sophia with my bare hands next time I saw her.

I went in the hotel and things did not get much better. I was taken into a basement bedroom, with no windows and very damp and humid. I turned round to the concierge and said.

"You are joking, right?; this can't be my bedroom?"

"Sorry, Mam, this is the only room left for the night; come and see me in the morning and I'll see where I can move you, but for now this is it, Mam"

As he left, I started to cry. It was the first time since I left London that I felt lonely. I sat on the bed and started to think of something positive: at least the room was quiet and as I was so tired, I soon fell asleep.

I woke up quite late due to the time difference and I quickly dressed up to go to reception only to find someone else there and me having to explain the situation all over again. He was very apologetic, and told me that the receptionist on the nightshift had given my room to somebody else thinking I wasn't turning up, instead of checking with the airline first, and I had been given a spare room offered only to staff. He apologized and gave me a suite and a free voucher for a massage. At least for now, Sophia's life had been spared. As soon as I left the hotel, the noise and the smells and the chaos just hit me like a bomb; I nearly went back to hide in my room as it was very daunting. I really began to question myself if the idea of travelling to India on my own was a good idea, but as I was already in the country and there was no going back, I took a deep breath and ventured my very first steps into this wild huge city only to jump into a sea of tourist touts all waiting for me like hungry hyenas, the porter of the hotel that was probably used to this scene grabbed my arm and pulled me back.

"Where do you want to go, Mam?"

"I just want to do a bit of sightseeing; see the Red Fort, India Gate, and all there is to see in Delhi".

"Let me arrange it with a taxi driver"

He went and talked to a taxi driver for quite a long time and then he opened the door for me.

"I told him to take you to all the places of interest and to take good care of you, Mam".

"Thank you". I gave him a tip and boarded the taxi.

"Good morning, Mam; we go to the Red Fort first, most famous in Delhi, Mam"

"What is your name?"

"Mr. Patel, Mam".

"In London, most Indian families are Patel"

"Yes, Mam, best name Mr Patel"

Mr Patel seemed like a nice decent man and at least inside the taxi I felt safe; he was very skinny and quite old but had a big smile and a happy disposition.

The road the hotel was in was chaotic but very colourful, full of street vendors and shops and restaurants and cows slowly walking amongst everything, so maybe when I got back, I could wonder around it. Driving around Delhi was quite something; the chaos wasn't just confined to the road the hotel was in but the whole city was a vast muddle of disorder and noise. The traffic was the worst I have ever witness and yet amongst it all, there was something magical about Delhi. The temples, the women wearing colourful saris, and the families of monkeys crossing the roads, all added to its charm. When we arrived at the Red Fort, I remembered all the period films made in India and how lavish they were. I wondered again if maybe I had lived here before although I didn't have the same feeling as I had in Istanbul. But I am sure I must have lived many lives and why not in India.

The hungry tourist hyenas were plentiful at the Fort but Mr Patel quickly got off the taxi and asked me to wait inside. He came back later with the entrance tickets and said he would be waiting for me when I came out. I wanted to pay him, but he would not have it.

"Later, later, Mam. At the end of the day you pay me, Mam".

I must have spent a couple of hours walking around the Fort and its beautiful grounds. When I returned to the taxi, Mr Patel was waiting with that infectious smile of his.

"Where do you want to go now, Mam?"

"I want to go and eat something please, Mr Patel; I am starving"

"Do you want European restaurant or Indian?"

"Indian restaurant; and please, Mr Patel, not a tourist place"

"Yes, Mam, Mr Patel will take you to best Indian restaurant in Delhi".

We arrived at a very crowded and noisy place. The restaurant had only benches like tables and we sat next to a very large family. They all turned round and smiled at me, they probably had not seen a tourist in that restaurant before and talked in Hindi to Mr Patel.

"Everything okay, Mr Patel?"

"Yes, yes, no problem, Mam; everything okay, Mam. What do you want to eat, Mam?"

"Something vegetarian, Mr Patel"

"I am vegetarian; I will order a selection of vegetarian dishes and some Nan bread. Is that okay with you, Mam?"

"That sounds lovely".

The food came all in a large tray and one tin plate for each of us. It did not look that great but when I put the first spoonful inside my mouth it tasted delicious; it transported me to another world.

"Wow, Mr Patel, this is delightful and not that hot, just wonderful and nothing like the Indian restaurants in London"

"Glad you like it, Mam"

The whole restaurant was looking at me; they all seemed pleased to see me enjoying the food.

That afternoon we just drove around Delhi, stopping at the India Gate, where everyone wanted a selfie with me. I later found out that Hindus love taking pictures with foreigners and posting them on Facebook. We also drove past the presidential palace and went into a couple of temples before returning to the hotel.

"Mr Patel, thank you for a wonderful day, please how much do I owe you?"

"In rupees or in pounds, Mam?"

"In pounds please", I said it expecting to pay a fortune

"That would be £20 Mam".

"And the entrance to the Fort and lunch?"

"That includes everything, Mam. Is that too much, Mam?" he said, without a smile on his face for the first time.

"No, Mr Patel, I think you must have made a mistake on the exchange rate. That is less than a short cab ride in London". I handed him £40 and left the taxi.

"Thank you, Mam, thank you".

"And you better be here tomorrow at 10am; there is lots more to see in Delhi that I want you to show me"

"Yes, Mam; no problem, Mam"

I went in the hotel and booked my free massage; I really wanted to relax after driving around Delhi all day long. There was an hour's wait so I decided to go and walk around the hotel's street. I took a deep breath and went for it; walking there was anything but a relaxing stroll; I had to be mindful of the rubbish, holes and dodge all sort of obstacles on the road. There was no footpath and if there was any, it was occupied by street vendors; there were also lots of tuck-tucks and motorbikes, not to mention the vast crowds of people and cows, but there was so much to see and take in, so colourful. Why can't women around the world all wear saris, so feminine and gorgeous; besides you can hide any extra bits under it all, no more dieting, beautiful and blissfully happy! I bought a few cotton loose clothes as I was feeling rather hot wearing my tight jeans. I started to understand why Sophia had recommended this hotel even though it was a far cry from the famous five-star Taj Mahal Hotel.

I went straight to the massage spa room when I returned from my adventure around the street. The lady that greeted me was very pleasant and welcoming, it was rather dark so I couldn't really see her features. She was wearing a green sari and the gold sparkled slightly with the reflection of the candles that lit the room; it smelt wonderful with the aroma coming out of the incense burners. I took my clothes off and laid down on the massage bed.

"Good afternoon, Mam; what kind of massage would you like to have, Mam?"

"Something relaxing; not too strenuous, please".

"I have Braham, Vishnu and Shiva massages; Braham is the most relaxing one and I use a mixture of soothing warm essential oils".

"Braham sound like heaven".

She put some relaxing music on and started pouring oil on my back; she then performed the most wonderful massage I had ever had.

The following day I went out at 10am and Mr Patel was waiting for me by the entrance door. His smile lit the whole road.

"Morning, Mr Patel".

"Morning, Mam, you look nice in Hindu Clothing".

"Thank you, Mr Patel; today I would like to go to a few more temples; maybe the Lotus Temple or Humayun's Tomb and I would love to visit a market".

"No problem, Mam; we can visit all, Mam".

We did go to all the temples and ended up with a visit to the Chandni Chowk market, a huge place filled with all types of shops, from spices to jewellery. I found it quite difficult to navigate and asked Mr Patel to take me back to my hotel. I thought it was better to venture around the local shops.

I asked Mr Patel if he could take me around the Golden Triangle to see Jaipur, Agra and the Taj Mahal and maybe go to Pushkar, as Sophia had told me it was very beautiful and worth going to. The whole trip would take a week and I could ask the hotel to help me out making hotel reservations.

"Yes, Mam, Mr Patel will make best price and trip for you, Mam".

We worked out the price and agreed that he would be there at 8am the following day to make an early start. I went in and made the hotel reservations and I was told that hotels provided rooms for the drivers, so I did not have to worry about that either.

I was out just after 8am and was surprised to see that Mr Patel wasn't there; I waited and waited and nothing. It never crossed my mind that he would not be there and I had not asked him for a contact number. And as most in India are called Patel, it would be impossible to try to find him. I went back to the hotel and explained the situation, and asked them to cancel the hotels. I was very worried that something might have happened to him.

"No need to cancel Mam, we can find you another driver straight away", said a new, much younger concierge that was now behind the counter. He signalled to a much younger but very serious driver that hurriedly stood up and came to me.

"Morning, Mam, I am Mr Kumar and I would have the privilege to be your driver for this trip".

I took a good look at him, and there was something that I did not like about him. I did not know how to explain it but something in my solar plexus did not feel right. It was just a gut feeling.

"Good morning, Mr Kumar, thanks for the offer but I still would like to wait for Mr Patel. I am sure he will be here soon. It must be down to Delhi's rush hour traffic".

I waited and waited and nothing; no Mr Patel.

The concierge and Mr Kumar approached me again and I reluctantly got into his taxi and set for Agra. I was really looking forward to the Taj Mahal and thought that maybe it was for the best; the taxi was quite a new car with full air conditioning but there was no infectious smile. After a very long and quiet journey, we arrived at the Taj Mahal. The usual tourist hyenas were waiting but this time I had to get out of the taxi all by myself and make my own way in; Mr Kumar did not make any effort to try to help me. It was hard to get through all the people at the entrance but once in the Taj Mahal it did not disappoint; it looks and feels even more majestic in real life, as the photographs do not convey the imposing grandeur and the vastness of the whole complex. I went in and had a picture taken in the same bench as Princess Diana had done all those years ago and I had the same feeling of loneliness as she probably had back then. There is a sad energy surrounding the Taj Mahal; it was commissioned by Shah Jahan in 1631 to be built in the memory of his favourite wife Mumtaz Mahal, who died giving birth to his fourteenth child. As I was walking around it, I slipped on the marble floors and the tile that I fell down into had the number 44 inscribed on it; the angel number; maybe they were looking after me or was it a warning from the angels? One thing was clear; I had to pay more attention to avoid slipping down again. I didn't want to end up in a hospital in India.

After the Taj Mahal, we set for Jaipur; I had booked a very nice hotel overlooking the Jal Mahal, a historic palace in the middle of a lake. When we arrived there, Mr Kumar could not find the hotel. We went up and down the road and he kept missing it. In the end he said he knew a very good hotel and that I would like it and it would probably be better than the one I had booked.

“Mr Kumar, I have already booked this hotel; it was recommended by the concierge at the Hari Park Hotel and I want to go there. Look here; let me stop a local taxi and I am sure he will be able to take us there”. And before he could say anything I got off the taxi and talked to a tuck-tuck driver.

“I am sure your driver knows how to get to your hotel; it's a very well-known hotel, but drivers do that to the tourist so they can take them to a hotel where they know they can get a good commission, so just be careful next time; it's a very old trick of the trade”.

I went back to my taxi and asked Mr Kumar to follow the tuck-tuck; I did not say anything, as I was very tired and just wanted to rest, but I was beginning to regret having agreed to Mr Kumar being my driver for this trip.

I woke up the following day to a beautiful view of the Tal Mahal, and now that I had time to rest, I realized what a beautiful hotel I was staying in and the difference with the Hari Park Hotel; it was more in accordance with I had imagined hotels in India would be like, probably influenced by all the Bollywood films I had watched over the years. I went to reception and asked the concierge if he could get me a tourist guide that could show me all the special places in Jaipur. I also explained what had happened with the driver the previous evening and did not want any more mishaps.

"We have a few guides here; would you like us to choose one?"

"Yes, please"

I was introduced to a few and I chose an older man quite similar to Mr Patel; he was a teacher and a part-time guide; his name was Mr Anand.

We went to meet Mr Kumar at the parking lot.

"Morning, Mr Kumar this is Mr Anand, he will be my tour guide here in Jaipur and you will take us wherever he says".

"Good morning, Mam; there was no need for a guide. I could have showed you around Jaipur, Mam"

"You couldn't even find the hotel last night and I don't want any more problems, so please do as he says".

"Yes, Mam", he said looking quite annoyed

Mr Anand sat in the front passenger seat and straight away Mr Kumar started talking to him in an angry tone in Hindi and I could see Mr Anand's face changing into a serious expression.

"Sorry, Mr Kumar, you will not talk in front of me in your own language".

"Yes, Mam", he said looking at me through the mirror.

I could sense that the taxi was beginning to feel like a battleground and that this was not going to be a very pleasant journey.

"Jaipur, the Pink City the capital of Rajasthan…" I could just hear Mr Anand's voice reciting Jaipur's history by heart; I was not quite paying attention to his words but just admiring the beautiful pink structures. When we arrived to the majestic Hawa Mahal, I said I wanted to get down and take some pictures; there were some lovely shops and I went into a few. I also noticed that every time I asked for something or the price of something Mr Kumar would talk to the shopkeeper first in Hindi; I also noticed that the prices were higher than in Delhi, and as I was trying not to haggle as Peter had said, I decided not to buy anything as some of the prices were way too high. We went for lunch and I sat by myself as I wanted to be on my own and I ordered just a few things but when the bill came, again I had to pay nearly London prices. I was very surprised at that as up to now India had been very cheap compared to the UK. After that I asked to be taken back to the hotel, I just wanted to enjoy the swimming pool and the views of the palace. I was beginning to worry about the prices of everything; if I kept spending money at this rate I was going to run out and be forced to return to London and start working again.

The following day we went to visit the Amber Fort, set on a hill a few kilometres from Jaipur. I noticed that there was the option of going up to the fort on elephant and I thought that would be a lovely idea. Mr Kumar quickly parked the car and went to talk to one of the elephant handlers. When I asked how much it would cost me, he gave a very high price, so I refused. I saw that there was a tourist kiosk, so I went and asked them was what a fair price and it turned out to be a fifth of the price the handler had given me, so I went back and confronted him.

"Sorry, Mam, your driver said it was for a family of five".

I looked at Mr Kumar and he said the man had probably misunderstood him and just turned round and left.

I went up to the Fort in the now fair priced ride but still with the feeling that something was not quite right. I spent as long as I could walking around this beautiful place; I didn't really want to go back to the taxi and Mr Kumar.

The following day I woke up early to drive to Pushkar, a Hindu pilgrimage town on a sacred lake. Sophia had said that this place was amazing and I was really looking forward to spending a few days there. Apparently, there were hundreds of temples, including one devoted to Brahma. That morning Mr Kumar was a bit more chatty than usual but I totally ignored him, I just did not trust him anymore and was using him as a means to an end but nothing else. On arrival at Pushkar there were the usual tourist hyenas waiting; this time Mr Kumar parked the car and escorted me around the town. I thought that maybe he had a change of heart. The town was full of shops selling all sorts of very colourful artefacts. I went in a few but Mr Kumar was always one step ahead of me talking to the owners first and as usual the prices were very steep. When we reached the Brahma temple, there were hundreds of guides offering to show you around and granting you direct access to the gurus. Mr Kumar introduced me to one that he said was a trusted friend of his, and as I was not quite sure of what to do, I accepted his offer. The guide showed me around everywhere and I was blessed by every guru in the temple and drenched in water using sacred water from the lake. When we came out, he charged me a fortune for his services and all the magic of the temple flew away in that transaction.

I asked Mr Kumar to take me to my hotel, and asked him to leave; I did not want him close to me at all. The hotel was on the river bank but on the other side of the town; it looked as it once it had been a grand colonial house now converted into a beautiful hotel. The room had very high ceilings, and a huge four-poster bed in the middle covered with lace; it looked amazing, shame I was alone and not just alone, I was feeling lonely. I wished I had waited for Mr Patel; I am sure I would have enjoyed everything about this amazing place a lot more.

At sunset the Gau Ghat temple has chants of prayer on the riverbank and people bathe in the holy water. I sat by the stairs and watched this awesome experience and tears started rolling down my cheeks; a very nice tall man came close to me and asked me if I was okay. I started really sobbing and told him everything that had happened since I left Delhi; the poor man listened to me and at the end gave me some water and invited me to have something to eat. We sat in the veranda on the hotel overlooking the lake, which looked even more beautiful at night with the reflexion of the city lights on its waters. He looked at me and smiled.

"Isn't it beautiful? I come here every evening and it never ceases to amaze me".

"Yes, it looks amazing. And the chanting brought me much needed peace".

"So, why be so sad? All that you have told me comes down to a very unfortunate common issue that tourist endure here in India: your driver is taking you for a ride. I see it all the time, he is selling you to the best bidder and taking commissions at every opportunity that he can manage. Change the driver".

"I wish I could, but I already paid for the whole package golden triangle tour at the hotel".

"Oh, dear, so sorry to hear that. So you are going to have to put up with him for a few more days".

"Nothing golden about this triangle; except the money the fucking driver has put in his pocket at my expense. Sorry about the fucking driver".

"No need to apologize, I would have called him far worse than that if I was being taken for a ride. At least let me show you around tomorrow; I will take you to all the temples here and will help you buy a few things without having to break your bank account and I won't charge you anything; all I want is to see you smile".

"Thanks for that; I would love you to show me around and not have to worry about how much I am worth".

"Can you please tell me your name so I know who to ask for in the morning?"

"Gaby, but you should ask for Gabriela Hall at reception. And yours?"

"Dev Patel".

"How come you don't call me Mam every five minutes like everyone here?"

"Would you like me to call you Mam?"

"Please don't, I am just wandering because you have been the first person here to treat me like a normal human being".

"I was brought up in London; although Southall is not exactly English, is more like an extension of India".

"How come you ended up living here?"

"When I finished school, I came here in search of my roots and I fell in love with this place, got married and never went back".

"So you are married?"

"My wife passed away, but I have two sons".

"I am sorry to hear that. Don't you ever think of going back?"

"I love my sons and my in-laws are helping me raise them; I could never take them away from them. But it's nice to be here with you so you can tell me all about cold, wet, and gloomy London".

"As long as you don't ask me about football or cricket, I am okay with that, but we better talk about it tomorrow as I am rather tired and will have plenty of time to talk about beautiful cool London".

"I'll be here around 9:30 am after I drop my children to school".

"See you tomorrow".

The following day Dev was at reception 9:30 am sharp; he asked me to point out Mr Kumar for him and he went straight towards him and gave him a big told off; all I could see was Mr Kumar bowing his head.

"I don't think he will be bothering you again".

"I wouldn't be so sure, I bet this is not the first time he has been caught red handed; I just don't trust him at all. I should have taken more notice of my gut feeling when I first met him. I knew that there was something not quite right with this man; I felt it right here in my solar plexus. This is a big lesson for me and I should follow my instincts in future".

"That's right, Gaby; people come all over the world to India is search of a "Guru" that can teach them all about life and enlightenment, when we are all our best teachers, we should listen more to ourselves, we have all the tools within us that can lead us to illumination, peace or whatever we are searching for in life".

"But there are good teachers here in India. I am going to Ranchi to the Ashram of Paramahansa Yogananda; a friend of mine recommended that place to me; she said it is a very special place".

"Paramahansa Yogananda was a great teacher; he was the first monk to travel to America and introduced millions of people to Kriya yoga. His book Autobiography of a Yogi has been my inspiration for life and one of the reasons I am living in India today. Have you read it?"

"Sorry, but no, I haven't"

"That's it; that is where we should start our tour today, I shall buy you a copy and you can read it while in the Ashram. You will like it there; it's a very peaceful place where you can meditate, go within you and find that inner peace that we all long for. You will then come to realize that we can make that space for ourselves anywhere we want to, wherever we are; we should all start our day with a mediation, but the Ashram is a good place to learn how to achieve that and besides there you can meet lots of lovely people. There is someone very dear to me living in the Ashram".

"There's something very special about you. You irradiate a peaceful soothing energy, that I have been feeling since I met you".

"It must be all those years of practicing yoga and meditation; that is why I am so happy here and I don't long for more, I found my own inner peace".

"I wish I could stay here with you and you could teach me how to find that peace".

"That is something I can't teach you; that is something that only you can teach yourself, but I can see that you are on the right path. So let's go and get you a copy of that book and afterwards I can take you to a few temples and we can meditate in some of them, but remember that the most sacred temple is your own body".

"You know what they say, When the student is ready the master appears, and I think you can be my master at least for the day".

Dev gave me a sweet look and off we went to buy my book and start our tour around the temples. There was something very special about Dave; the way he walked was so serene and graceful; he looked as if he was floating. I could only relax and enjoy his company. He had managed to vanish all the anger I had due to Mr Kumar's behaviour, and probably if it was not for him, I would not have met this beautiful man, so as they all say, there are no coincidences in life as this was meant to be, even if it had caused me so much anger.

We walked into the first temple, a small quite hidden place; we left our shoes by the entrance and Dev lead me to a small shrine. There were hardly any people there, quite a huge contrast with the overcrowded places that Mr Kumar had taken me to the previous day. Dev sat cross-legged and I copied him; we closed our eyes and a few minutes later a monk came in, he sat in front of the shrine and started to chant some mantras. Dev joined in the chanting and I just sat there quietly, taking it all in. The energy that I felt there reminded me of the evening prayer in Fátima. I had goose pins; tears started rolling down my cheeks, and an overwhelming feeling of peace started flowing all over me. For a few minutes I was transported into an altered high state unlike anything I had felt before. Once the chanting stopped, the monk stood up and left the room. Dev looked at me and signal me to also stand up and leave.

"That was so lovely, Dev; and what a beautiful small temple".

"I have been coming every morning here for many years; it's hidden from the tourist and it's one of the only true Buddhist temples here in Pushkar; you will have to go to the Himalayas to find really good authentic temples and monks, but for me this is where I come and find my peace every day".

"For a few minutes there I felt this immense feeling of peace; it was very overwhelming".

"That is exactly what I was talking you about earlier on; no one can do that for you, you have to do the work yourself".

"Yes, but sitting next to you helped a lot as it did the energy of the whole place and the chanting".

"The chanting helps to raise the energy and allows you to get into those alter states; if you go to the Himalayas were lots of monks do the morning prayers together, you will understand what I mean".

"Let's have a cup of tea and you can tell me all about the temples in the Himalayas; maybe I can go there after visiting the Ashram".

We walked to a small cafe and we sat in the balcony with a splendid view of the lake, there was a cool breeze and it was just perfect.

"Sitting here I understand why you don't want to leave this place, but I am not sure I can stay here forever".

"I have my roots here now and I make a good living sending all sorts of items to a shop that me and my brother have in Southall; I am the buyer and my brother looks after the shop, so it's a win, win situation. But for me the most important thing in life is to grow spiritually. I believe we come to this earth just for that, but most people get tangled up with day to day survival and get consumed trying to acquire things, when all we need to is attain spiritual growth; it's the only thing that matters and the only thing we can carry with us to the other side".

"Unfortunately, for most people life is a struggle; paying bills and keeping their head above water is not easy".

"You can do all that and still have time for meditation there must be a balance in life and all it takes is just a few minutes every morning, just as we brush our teeth on a daily basis, we can sit quietly for a short while. Give it a try it; will change your life for the better, and you don't have to become a monk in order to be enlightened; there is always a lesson to gain during our daily life existence".

"I was tangled up in my daily routine back in London and one day I decided I had enough and took a sabbatical and started traveling and since I started, I have been mindful of things that have been happening to me. And yes, I have learnt a lot about life and things and teachers have been appearing in my life as if by magic, just like you did".

"You see, when the student is ready the teacher appears, but you are your best teacher; bear that in mind always, people may appear in your life and give you a helping hand but, you have to do the work yourself, no one can ever do it for you!!"

I gave him my best smile and thought of all the people that just want someone to appear with a magic wand and fix everything in life for them.

And as if reading my mind Dev said,

"There is no magic wand!"

I just thought to myself, I better do not think of anything bad as he can surely read my mind.

"Come on; let's go, there is a lot more I want to show you".

We spent all afternoon visiting many temples of all faiths and just walking around Pushkar; at about 4pm he said he had to go and pick up his children from school. So sadly, I had to say goodbye to this beautiful soul, which had taught me so much in such a short time.

And again, as if reading my mind, he said

"Is not the amount of time we spend with someone; is the quality of time we give them; it's been an absolute pleasure spending the day with you even if we never spoke about wet and gloomy London".

"The pleasure it's been all mine, even if we never talked about the temples in the Himalayas and thank you for everything, I will never forget you",

I gave him a big hug trying to squeeze all the knowledge and goodness out of this man that had crossed my path to teach me so much.

The following day Mr Kumar was waiting at the door of the hotel with a big smile on his face as if nothing had happened.

"Where to Mam? Are we going to do the camel ride or visit another fort that is not too far from here?"

"No, Mr Kumar we are going back to Delhi"

"But Mam, you still have another evening booked at the hotel".

"Mr Kumar, I am done with you, and I want to go back to Delhi".

"Yes, Mam"

We set back to Delhi; I did not want to spoil the wonderful memories of the time I had in Pushkar with Dev Patel.

It was a long journey and we stopped in a road restaurant to have lunch; I ordered something and then I noticed that Mr Kumar was back to his old tricks talking to the owner of the restaurant. When the bill came it was very expensive, so I asked to see the menu and I compared prices: everything had been doubled. I made a list of my dishes and added it all up, went to the till and the man apologised; he said that it was Mr Kumar's idea and that the rest of the dishes were his lunch. I said I would only pay for mine and that he could send the bill to Mr Kumar for him to pay for his. When I got back into the car, he was trying to excuse himself saying he only did it to pay for his children's school. I said I would have given him a huge tip if he had behaved properly and to please shut up.

It was rush hour when we arrived at Delhi and we had to crawl all the way until we reached the hotel. If people in London thought that rush hour traffic was bad, they should come and spend one minute in Delhi. I swear to God I will never, ever complain again. The noise, the horns, the tuck-tucks, bikes, the dust, the cows, the monkeys, all happening at the same time, I do not know how anyone can survive living through this every day.

Mr Patel was waiting for me sitting in the stairs in front of the hotel; he had a cast in one of his arms and a bandage on his forehead.

"Ms Gaby, are you okay Mam?"

"I am Okay, Mr Patel but what happened to you?"

"I had an accident that morning when I was coming to pick you up; I tried calling the hotel but they wouldn't put me through to you. I was very worried and was trying to warn you about bad drivers and when I heard you had gone with Mr Kumar I was really concerned; he is the worst of them all, and I have been waiting for you to return to apologize, Ms Gaby".

"There is no need to apologize Mr Patel.

I soon found out about Mr Kumar's tricks and a very nice man in Puskar helped me out, but from now on, you and only you will drive me around Delhi".

"But I only have a tuck-tuck now, the car is being fixed".

"Then we will have to go around in your tuck-tuck; I will love to experience that. Make sure you are here early tomorrow morning; I am flying in the evening to

Ranchi, so we have to make the most of my time left here in Delhi".

"See you tomorrow, Mam, and wait for me please".

"See you tomorrow, Mr Patel"

I went to the hotel and I asked to talk to the manager. I told him everything that had happened with Mr Kumar and that he had been recommended by the young concierge that was at reception that morning.

"That would have been my nephew. I would really like to apologize and may I offer you another free massage and dinner on my behalf? Please, Mam".

"Thank you, but please don't ever use Mr Kumar again and say something to your nephew. If he is going to be working in your hotel this is not the way to treat your clients, it's not good for your reputation. I could post it all over social media and some may go even further and do a lot of damage to the hotel".

"Yes, Mam, please accept my apologies, Mam".

As soon as I turned round, I heard the manager shouting at someone on the phone, probably his nephew; let's hope he got the message. Later on, in bed I felt in heaven and thought that after all I had a lot to thank Mr Kumar for.

Early the following morning Mr Patel was waiting for me by the front door in his tuck-tuck.

"Morning, Ms Gaby; ready to have the best experience in Delhi?" Mr Patel asked bearing that contagious smile of his.

"I'm not sure if I will ever be ready for a ride in a tuck-tuck but I trust you", I said smiling back at him, but thought to myself that I was probably mad to be getting in a tuck-tuck in Delhi with a man that had a cast on one arm. But off we went, OMG!; this was worse than being in a bumper car ride at the funfair. I was holding on for dear life; from time to time, Mr Patel turned around looking at me with his big smile.

"Don't worry, Ms Gaby; I am the best tuck-tuck driver in Delhi".

We stopped in a few more temples and in each one I prayed to God to let me enjoy another day and survive my day around Delhi. But survive I did and he even dropped me off at the airport safe and sound, after giving him a huge hug and a massive tip.

Ranchi

I ventured into Delhi's airport; it looked more chaotic than the streets of Delhi, after a bit of a struggle I manage to locate Air India's counter only to find out everybody screaming and complaining. My flight had been cancelled! I stood there not knowing what to do; I joined in the queue pushing my way through until I reached the counter only to be told by the Air India's representative that all he could offer me was a flight in the 20:20 IndiGo flight that would get me into Ranchi at 22:15. It was later that I would have liked to arrive but the alternative was spending one more night in Delhi and to be honest I didn't fancy staying another minute at the Hari Park Hotel. I checked in and found myself a seat where I could start reading my new book, The Autobiography of a Yogi. The time passed but just before I was supposed to board my flight, I heard from the loudspeakers that the flight had been delayed, meaning I would be arriving even later than planned. I tried calling the ashram but had no luck in getting through to them; all I could do was wait. Finally, we were called to board the flight. While in the queue I noticed a lady staring at my book and then she said to me.

"I love that book; in fact, I am flying to Ranchi to go to his Ashram"

"OMG, me too; thank God for that, I can't believe it", I dropped my things to the floor and gave this lady a big hug.

"I'm Gaby, lovely to meet you".

She gave me a big hug too. "I'm Rita; it looks as if Yogananda is working his magic already. I am so pleased to see you. I come all the way from New York and after all the delays I am exhausted and was dreading arriving so late by myself to the Ashram".

The flight to Ranchi took nearly 2 hours so we landed nearly at mid night. Rita and me took a taxi to the Ashram but when we arrived there, everything was dark. We asked the driver to put the lights on and he started honking until eventually a monk came to open the gate.

"Good evening, ladies; we thought you weren't coming as we found out your flight had been cancelled", said the monk sounding very apologetic".

"We were booked on a later flight and we did try to phone you but we couldn't get through", I retorted to the monk.

"The telephone connection has been down throughout the day as they are trying to fix a damage somewhere along the line; sorry about it, but please come in, I will show you to your room".

The room was a very basic one, with two single beds, all very clean and neat; the beds had four aluminium posters to hang the mosquito nets from and a ceiling fan.

"The toilet facilities are at the end of the corridor and the bell will ring five minutes before prayer starts. Namaste!", said the monk bowing his head.

"I am going to take a shower before I go to sleep", I said to Rita, and I took a towel and my dressing gown

I came back to the room a bit later bursting with laughter

"OMG! There is no shower, just a tap and a bowl and the toilet is just a hole in the ground, so brace yourself for it".

"Oh, no; I was hoping I could have a long warm shower, oh well, I better have a go at this bowl thing then. I can see this is going to be a challenge".

I was so tired that I went straight to sleep and did not even hear Rita coming back into the room.

Early in the morning I was woken up by the sound of a loud bell ringing in the corridor just outside our bedroom. I looked at Rita and she had her pillow over her head, so I assumed she didn't want to get up for the morning prayer. I quietly put on some Indian cotton clothing and slipped out of the bedroom. As I closed the door, there were a few other people leaving their rooms.

"Namaste".

"Namaste".

I followed them as I didn't have a clue were to go. We left the building that housed the bedrooms and walked across beautiful lush gardens, covered with mature trees and green tropical plants and flowers.

The noise of the birds singing was very loud and cheerful; we reached a large white building and inside there was a very large room with a purpled patterned carpet and lots of pillows. I sat cross-legged in on one of the pillows in front of a shrine that had a large picture of Paramahansa Yogananda adorned with gold and red garlands and a candle on each side. I waited for a while until four monks came into the room; two of them were wearing yellow robes and the other two orange ones. They sat down in front of some musical instruments, some of which I had never seen before; one of the monks said a few words in English welcoming the new arrivals and then he continued talking in Hindi. I didn't understand anything but his voice was very soothing; he lit the candles and incense burner and as he did this, he lashed his back gently with a sort of mop, he then started a guided meditation both in English and in Hindi.

"As we begin our meditation it is important to sit in the correct posture with our backs straight and the chin parallel to the floor. Close your eyes and gently lift your gaze to the point between the eyebrows; mentally command the body to be still and relax, consciously feel the body relaxing, let go of all cares and concerns and feel the peace within. Let us begin with a prayer; please repeat after me: Oh, spirit teach me to find thy presence, in the joy that springs from deep meditation. Ommmmm, Ommmmm, Ommmmm".

At this point all the monks joined in and started to play the instruments and sing some beautiful mantras; the whole atmosphere was electrifying. After a while they kept quiet. By then we were all in a state of deep meditation and all that we could hear was the deep breathing of all the people in the room, but after a while all we could hear was the rambling of my stomach I had not eaten for a long time and I was beginning to feel really hungry. I think the monk must have heard me or read my thoughts because he then made a final short prayer.

"You can now gently open your eyes and may you have a peaceful day".

"Breakfast will be ready in a few minutes; make sure you are in the dining room shortly".

I followed everyone through the garden into another building and there was a large dining room that reminded me of my school days. Everybody was queuing up and behind the counter, there were some people serving breakfast. At this point, I realized that Rita was not in the place so I quickly went back to our bedroom to find her.

She was still asleep but I thought it was best to wake her up.

"Morning, Rita; is time to wake up"

She gently opened her eyes.

"Is it time for morning prayer?"

"I am afraid you missed the morning prayer but it's time for breakfast now and we better don't miss it as it's been a while since we last ate anything".

Rita quickly put something on and we ran to the dining room; we were the last two on the queue but we made it. The food was served in aluminium plates and it consisted of a very basic porridge with some fruit and nuts topping it and a cup of green tea. Rita's jaw dropped in disbelieve.

"That's all?"

"I am afraid that is all, you will get used to it. This breakfast will give you the energy you need and as we spend most of the day in deep meditation, we don't need much to keep us going. I gather you are new arrivals?"

"Yes, we arrived late last night; our flight was much delayed".

"If you want to, I can show you around after breakfast. I can take you to complete your registration and I can show you the grounds and tell you a bit about the history of the place".

"That would be wonderful", said a pleased Rita.

"I didn't catch your name", I said to our new friend.

"I'm Anika; pleased to meet you"

We finished our breakfast and Anika was waiting by the door. She was a very slim, blond lady that looked like Scandinavian, very posed and graceful. We followed her out of the dining room and through the gardens and into the reception area. She registered both of us and then asked us to give a donation for our stay.

"As you know the Ashram doesn't charge for accommodation or food but if you can please help with a donation. Anything that you can help the Ashram is very welcome as it's the only way to keep the place going".

I took a £ 50 note and Rita a US$ 100. Anika looked very pleased and put the notes in a safety box.

"This is a list of chores that you can also help out with", said Anika showing us quite a long list of everyday jobs: cleaning, cooking, dishwashing, gardening, washing, welcoming new arrivals. Well, now I knew what Anika's job was. I wrote my name next to washing dishes and Rita wrote hers next to gardening.

"Thank you for your help, ladies. Now we can start the tour. As you might already know, it was here in Ranchi, in 1917, that Paramahansa Yogananda began his life's work with the founding of an ashram and a "How-to-Live" school for boys, and to make available the universal teachings of Kriya Yoga. This is Paramahansa Yogananda' Room; his living quarters during the early years is preserved as a shrine. The room is open to all for private meditation throughout the day. You can see that here we have the hand and foot impressions of the Guru brought from the SRF International Headquarter in Los Angeles, California".

We then walked outside into the gardens. It was a scorching hot morning and I was quite relieved I did not choose gardening as I thought that between the sun and the mosquitoes it could be quite a hard job. We stood in front of a very large tree that had a big picture of Yogananda under it.

"This is the Litchi Vedi; is one of the sacred places here in the Ranchi Ashram. It was under the shady canopy of this large litchi tree that the great Guru frequently held outdoor classes and Satsang's and it still one of the favourite places for people to come and meditate".

We kept walking around the gardens until we reached a tall hexagonal marble temple with decorative lace wall on all the sides and a large lotus dome.

"This is the Smriti Mandir, a memorial to the world wide mission that took its first step here in Ranchi. And this is the end of our tour; you are welcome to wonder around the Ashram. And remember our next guided meditation is at 12 o'clock in the main hall, followed by lunch, then a light dinner at 6 followed by a long evening meditation".

I walked towards the Litchi Vedi and sat under the tree trying to meditate but mostly thinking about Yogananda and all the times he must had spent meditating under this same tree; it was very relaxing sitting there listening to the birds and refreshed by a light cool wind. A while later I heard the bell ringing and I saw lots of people from all the corners of the Ashram walking towards the main hall for the mid-day guided meditation. This time there was only one monk dressed in orange robes that guided the meditation; it was much shorter and I was quite relieved as I was starving and found it quite hard to relax while my stomach was making all the usual rumbling hungry noises. After it was over, I followed everyone to the dining room hoping to find a big spread of yummy food, only to find the same sort of small portions we had for breakfast: a small spoonful of rice and dahl, with a nan bread. I am not very fond of eating carbs, but if I did not eat the rice and bread, I would probably end up fainting by the end of the day. I saw Rita at a distance looking with disbelieve at her plate; we had split after the tour; she had stayed with Anika when I went to the gardens

After lunch I went to do my daily core of dishwashing and afterwards, I went to my room. I was feeling a bit tired and really wanted to have a nap but as soon as I lay down on my bed, and before I could even close my eyes, Rita burst into the room:

"I must tell you all about this place. Anika has been living her for a whole year and she told me everything about it".

"No wonder she is so slim", I said quite sarcastically

Rita completely ignored me and just kept talking and talking; her voice only made me more tired and soon I closed my eyes and fell asleep.

I woke up later on that evening only to find Rita fast asleep in her bed. I had a good look at the bedroom and she had managed to make a mess of the whole place already her clothes were scattered everywhere while my belongings were neatly tucked away under my bed. I was beginning to regret having to share the bedroom with her; I am not used to sharing anything and the one thing that I had found most difficult throughout my sabbatical was the lack of privacy. I quietly slipped out of the room as I did not want Rita to wake up and continue telling me all about the Ashram. I went straight to the dining room, as I did not want to waste any opportunity to have any food, but there was just one thing on offer: a very watered down vegetable soup. Well, at least there were not going to be too many dishes to wash up after the meal.

The evening meditation was guided by three monks all dressed in yellow robes, and it turned out to be a prayer more so than a guided meditation. We gave thanks for everything and sent peace to all corners of the world. The monks left and whoever wanted to stay could spend as much as she or he wanted mediating there. I stayed another half an hour or so but the sound of the ceiling fans was making me sleepy and I went to my bedroom. Rita was still fast asleep. I took my towel and pyjamas, went to the washroom, and found Anika also there. I washed myself as best as I could and was getting ready to go back to my room when Amika asked me:

"Would you like a cup of tea and cookies?"

"I would love some biscuits", I said nearly pleading with her to give me some food.

"I know it can be difficult at the beginning as we are not used to so very little food, but it does get easier. In general we eat far too much and that is why there is so much obesity in the world. You will find that with very little of the right food we do start to function better and be less tired. We don't get tired due to not eating enough but due to eating too much and specially the wrong foods. Then our poor body have to battle to process it all and the only way it can do it is if it gets us tired and sends us to sleep as it's the easiest way to get rid of it all".

"But I have been feeling tired and sleepy here and I've hardly eaten anything".

"That is only while the body adjusts and due to the heat, but give it a few days and you will begin to feel better, I promise you that".

We walked to her bedroom; it was very homely, full of rugs and Indian ornaments. She had a few candles lit and I found it very cosy. She had in a corner of the room a small makeshift kitchen and a kettle and in front of it there was a table and two chairs. We sat at the table and she brought me a cup and a few herbal teas for me to choose from.

"Rita told me you had been living here for a year".

"Almost two years now".

"What makes you stay here for so long?"

"I don't have anything or anyone to go back to".

"How come?"

"My only daughter died in a car accident two years ago; I eventually split up from my husband and lost my job and my will to live. A friend suggested I should come here, I took a plane and I have been living here ever since".

"But you can't hide here the rest of your life".

"Maybe one day I will go back but I have no intentions of doing so just yet. I have found peace here and my Mum and my sister have visited me here twice already. I've heard my ex-husband has remarried and I can't think of having to go back and earn a living and face the world". I saw a tear rolling down her face so I changed the subject not to press her anymore. I asked her about life outside the Ashram's walls.

"Ranchi is as chaotic as the rest of India; there is a small shopping area not far from here that sells all sorts of costume jewellery and scarves that are good priced if you want to buy something for your friends back home. However, I wouldn't recommend much going out; it's better to spend your time here in the Ashram mediating and disconnecting from the outside world".

I thanked for the tea and biscuits and left.

"Namaste".

"Namaste".

Rita was still fast asleep; no doubt, the jetlag had finally caught up with her. I quietly went into my bed and soon dozed off, only to be woken up by the morning bell, to start the daily routine all over again. Rita could not believe that she had missed the evening meal and mediation. I told her that she had not missed much but it was better if we hurried up before we missed breakfast. She was searching all over the messed-up bedroom trying to find her underwear and I soon left before it got frantic.

"See you soon, hope you find your clothes, bye". I closed the door and quickly left before she could say anything.

I went to the breakfast room and mainly looked at all the people that were there. We came from all corners of the world and different backgrounds, but everyone there was searching for that peace and happiness that seems to elude us all.

We finished our morning meditation and went for a walk around the gardens. There I saw Rita sweating it out in the morning heat making holes in the garden, while the head gardener was telling her just to dig a bit deeper. I had to stop and laugh; when she saw me laughing, she gave me the look….

Later on in our room she came in and sat on the bed with a very long face.

"This is not what I imagined it would be; I've dreamt all my life of coming here but I wasn't expecting it to be this hard: no shower, no food, and having to dig holes in the middle of this freaking heat".

"What we need is to go shopping. Anika told me that not too far from here there are very good shops. Let's go out for a minute; maybe the change of scenery will do us good".

"That sounds like a good idea". She gave the biggest smile I had seen from her since we arrived at the Ashram. Nothing like a bit of shopping therapy to brighten a girl's heart.

As soon as we set foot out of the Ashram, I felt like I was stepping out of the Hari Park Hotel: the noise, the dust, the cows, the million bikes and cars and tuck-tucks.

"Welcome to India", I said to Rita.

"This can't be right; this is a nightmare"

"Don't panic; it's not as bad as it looks. Let's take a tuck-tuck; they are amazing".

I stopped one and a nice old man with a big smile that reminded me of Mr Patel asked us where we wanted to go.

"I was told there are a few shops not far from here".

"The shops are just two minutes away from here. I better take you for a ride around the town and then I can drop you of there".

"That sound like a great idea".

Ranchi was bigger than I expected it to be. The driver took us to a hill where we could have a good view of the city and drove us past in front of a few temples and places of interests. As it was lunch hour we asked him to take us to a good place where we could have good local food. We ate as if we had never eaten before in our lives and the food tasted delicious. During lunch the driver told us that Ranchi was famous for its ethnic handicrafts and jewellery and that the best place to buy them was at the Firayalal, one of the most popular shopping destinations, that was not far from the Ashram. He mentioned that he himself visited the Ashram and he had taken many pilgrims there to buy gifts. After lunch he dropped us to do our shopping. We asked him to pick us up in an hour's time to take us back to the Ashram. The place was indeed full of beautiful things to buy; I thought about Linda and my friends back in London and bought a few things for them. When I next saw Rita, she had two big bags full and a huge smile.

"This is the best shop ever; I'll have to come here again. But now I have to go to an ATM machine as I have run out of money and we still have to pay the driver".

"Don't worry I can pay today; you'll pay him next time".

"But it will probably cost us a lot of money".

"Trust me it won't. And we better get back before the evening meditation".

The driver was waiting for us just outside the front door; he still had his big smile and we were also pleased to see him.

"Back to the Ashram please; we are going to miss the evening meditation and we already missed the lunch one".

We arrived and I asked him:

"How much do we owe you and please can we have your name and a mobile number so we can call you if we need to?"

"1.000 rupees, please".

I handed him the money and he gave me a card with his name and number. Mr Patel, I should have guessed it. Rita came running behind me:

"How much was that in dollars?"

"That's £10 pounds; in dollars about $13"

"For driving us all day and waiting for us, and lunch?"

"I told you it wouldn't break our bank account".

"This has been a great day, thank you, I really needed it".

We rang the bell and we waited and waited until finally a monk came to open the door. He did not look too pleased to see us.

"Please come in; next time if you want to go out please inform us; we were waiting for you. Gaby you are supposed to wash the dishes after meals and Rita, you only did very little garden work and then you disappeared and besides if you want to come and stay at the Ashram, we really want you to spend all the time here meditating, stepping out from the outside world".

"Namaste".

"Namaste".

Rita and I went quickly to our room and as soon as we closed the door, we burst out laughing.

"Oh, dear, I feel like being back at school" I said to Rita.

"But the escape was really worth it and we better go to the mediation room before we get another scolding".

We went to the meditation room and I just couldn't relax; I kept thinking about my time in Pushkar with Dev Patel; how amazing and easy it was to meditate with him. He seemed like a real enlightened man, but what I liked the most about him was the balance he had between his spiritual life and his daily living. I don't believe that we have to become monks or nuns in order to become enlightened or be a true spiritual being; I do believe that we can have a balance and Dave Patel had found it in Pushkar. I thought I would call him in the morning and ask him about the Himalayas, as I thought it would be the best place for me to spend the last few weeks of my sabbatical.

As soon as I had finished washing dishes after breakfast, I went to my bedroom to call Dev.

"Hello, Dev; it's me Gaby calling you from Ranchi"

"Hello, Gaby, how is everything going?"

"This is a very beautiful place; love the gardens and plenty of meditations..." And before I said anything else he added:

"But".

"But this is not for me", I said with a sigh of relief.

"I suppose it's too restrictive for you".

"Exactly; I feel like I am back at school. We even got told of because we ventured outside the Ashram one day".

"Who is we?"

"Me and my roommate Rita".

"I see; so what can I do for you?"

"We can have the conversation we never had about the Himalayas. I would love to go there but I haven't got a clue of where to go or anything about them".

"You have two options: you can go to Dharmsala, where the Dalai Lama lives; you have to bear in mind that he is not often there and you have to book somewhere to stay beforehand as it's a popular destination. Or you can fly to Leh in Ladakh. You will need a guide there; I have a very good friend and fantastic guide; his name is Stanzin Sangdup. He knows all the monasteries in the region and he will find you the best places to stay. I will text you his details later; you better send him a message, I will also let him know that I have given his number to you. There is hardly any internet connection up in the Himalayas, so it might take a few days before he replies and he might be busy, I do not know. But I'll suggest you try and contact him first and if that doesn't work go to Dharmsala".

"Thanks for that, Dev. I'll let you know how it goes".

"Try and enjoy your stay in Ranchi; there is a lot of good energy there; try and keep true to yourself".

"I will and thanks".

"Namaste".

I texted Stanzin and went to the gardens. I found myself a quiet spot under the canopy of some trees and for the first time since I arrived here in Ranchi, I really let myself go and I had a nice relaxing meditation. I could feel Dev's energy there with me, it was as if listening to his southing voice had changed my perception of this place; maybe I was expecting too much and talking to Dev reminded me that it's me and not the place that can bring magic into my life.

It took another day for Stanzin to reply:

"Dear Gaby, I am busy with clients until Sunday when I will drop them at the airport in Leh at 2pm and then I can pick you up. I am free for the next 2 weeks; let me know if that is okay for you".

I was so happy I went straight to my room to try to find flights to Leh. There were no direct flights; I would need to fly back to Delhi and take a connecting flight. I booked my flights and sent a text to Stanzin: "Stanzin, arriving in Air India flight from Delhi at 4pm on Sunday; please book a place for me to stay on arrival. See you soon, Gaby".

I was over the moon that I would be travelling to the Himalayas; it felt as if I was going to a magical place and could not wait for Sunday to arrive. Now I had to tell Rita. I did not want her to come with me; she is very nice but something about her messy lifestyle did not agree with me, it drained my energy. I was about to close my laptop when Rita burst into my room.

"What are you up to?"

"I was booking a flight to Leh for this Sunday".

"Where on earth is Leh and what are you going to do there?"

"Leh is in Ladakh, in the Himalayas".

"What are you going to do in the Himalayas?"

"I am not sure. Dev the man a met in Pushkar recommended it to me, so I am going there".

"Just like that without doing any research or finding more about the place; I could never travel like that, it took me two years to investigate about this place and India. I am going to Varanasi afterwards, it's meant to be the holiest place in India, on the banks of the river Ganges".

"I am following my gut feeling. And besides, I trust Dev".

"But you only met this guy for one day; you are absolutely crazy. Good luck with your journey".

I gave her a big smile and left the room. And to think that I had even worried about telling her…

I went to Paramahansa Yogananda's Room. I sat there and I noticed that Anika was also in the place. She was deep in contemplation, yet she had tears rolling down her cheeks. It broke my heart; I do not think one can ever recover from losing a child. I closed my eyes but after a short while I felt someone tapping at my shoulder; it was Anika. I stood up and followed her to her room or I might say home. It was such a peaceful place; I just wished she could one day find that same peace within herself.

"The pain of losing my daughter never goes away".

"I can't even begin to imagine what that must be like; but let's talk about nice things. I am traveling to Leh on Sunday; I am going to visit some monastery's there and see the majestic and mysterious Himalaya; you never know; I might find Shambala".

"One day I might go too. How come are you going there?"

"I met a guy in Pushkar, Dev Patel; such an enlightened human being".

"I know Dev; he's been here a few times".

"Yes, he was the one that bought me Paramahansa Yogananda's book, the Autobiography of a Yogi. But he also mentioned the Himalayas and somehow that appeals more to me as if I have been travelling all this way just to go there".

"Dev Patel, that's a man I would probably leave this place for".

"OMG, you are the one he must have referred too when he said that there was someone very dear to him living in the Ashram; you two would be perfect together, why don't you go and visit him?"

"The thought has crossed my mind and he has invited me many times, but I have never had the courage to do so".

"That's it! You are travelling with me on Sunday to Delhi and I have the best person to drive you all the way to Pushkar: another Mr Patel and I am sure you will never regret it".

"But I don't think I can afford it".

"Nothing will give me more pleasure than to buy your passage back into the real world and to bring a sparkle back into Dev Patel's life".

I ran back to my room and grabbed my laptop; my adrenalin was overflowing and my brain was working overtime. I had this feeling that maybe this was one of the main reasons I had come to Ranchi: to get these two together; there are definitely no coincidences in life. I thought maybe it was best to tell Dev, just to make sure he was going to be in Pushkar and that he was okay with it all.

"I can't believe this is happening; you have finally managed to do what I have been dreaming for so long. And don't even think about sending her with a driver; I'll come and pick her up from Delhi", was Dev's replay when I asked him.

"Great, that will give me a chance to say goodbye to you".

"It will never be goodbye; I am sure we will meet again, maybe in London with Anika".

"I'll text you the flight details once I've done the booking".

I rushed back to Anika's bedroom and before she could say anything, I booked her on the flight to Delhi on the seat right next to mine. I texted Dev and sat back relaxing, enjoying my cup of tea, beaming with happiness, knowing that I had done something really good. I was igniting the sparkle back in Dev's and Anika's lives. I was sitting there feeling good about myself and Anika was in a state of panic.

"What am I going to wear?"

"That is the million dollars question all women around the world want an answer for and one that all men around the world don't care at all".

We both burst out laughing

"Do you really think that Dev Patel is going to see you at the airport, look at your clothes and say, "No, go back I am not having you wearing that!" He is going to be there to see you, the real you, the one he probably fell in love the first minute he saw you; has he ever seen you wearing anything besides the clothes you always wear here?"

"No, but I still want him to see me nice".

"You are nice just the way you are but I get your point: women, we are all the same; we worry too much and give too much credit to clothes, when it's just what we have inside those clothes that we should really be worrying about. But let's go to the shopping centre and get you some new clothes and maybe go to the hairdresser and get you a new haircut".

That got Anika all happy; she changed her sad look in her face with a more content one. Even if it is not what men want, clothes and shopping for new ones does make women happier and going to the shops today was going to be worth it even if we got a reprimand later on. I called my trusted tuck-tuck driver and off we went. Anika tried lots of clothes. She looked lovely in everything she tried on; in the end we bought three new outfits, Indian style clothes, not saris but loose and colourful. Then we went to the hairdressers to give some life back to that long dreary hair that probably had not seen a pair of scissors since she landed in India and reshape of her eyebrows, wax, nails and three hours later Anika looked 10 years younger and stunningly beautiful.

When we finally arrived at the Ashram, the monk that opened the door was gobsmacked. He didn't say anything; he couldn't take his eyes of her, and he ran back to tell the other monks who all came to take a good look at the new Anika. They all looked very pleased to see her so radiantly beautiful and happy, and when we told them that she was going away on Sunday they were static. I think they never thought that day would come; they had grown to love her but they also wanted her to be happy on her own away from the Ashram.

Sunday arrived and we said our goodbyes; all Rita wanted was to move into Anika's bedroom; she was probably going to be the next permanent resident in the Ashram but I knew that the beautiful peaceful sanctuary that Anika's had created would be destroyed in five minutes once Rita moved in.

Anika was very nervous throughout the flight; I am sure that if she could have opened the door and ran back to the safety of the Ashram she would have done so. But as soon as we landed and she saw Dev looking at her as soon as the exit airport doors opened, I am sure that in that instance the Ashram became just a distant memory. And when I saw them embraced in pure love I couldn't stop crying. I had never felt so much love in my life and I though right then if I was ever going to share my life with someone it would have to feel just like that.

Dev gave me a hug and just said:

"Thank you".

"The pleasure is totally mine", I said with a big smile on my face. He handed me a rucksack.

"Do you mind taking this to Stanzin; these are gifts for his children".

"I'm sure I can take an extra bag on board; I have already forwarded my luggage to my connecting flight".

I watched as they vanished in the distance, walking together to a beautiful future ahead.

Himalayas

I boarded my connecting flight to Leh, sat by the window and just stared outside as the plane took off towards the highest chain of mountains in the world. My heart was pounding and I had butterflies in my stomach as if I was going to meet up with the love of my life. An hour into our flight the pilot announced that from the right-hand side of the plane it was possible to see some of the eight-thousanders, or mountains that are more than 8,000 metres in height, and as it was my lucky day, it was my side of the plane. At a distance, I could see the majestic mountain tops visible just above the clouds. What a glorious sight! One that I shall never forget, to see Mount Everest, Makalu, Lhotse, Cho Oyu and a few more in one go was a dream come true and it was even more impressive when the pilot said that it was a very rare view as they were usually covered by the clouds. The plane flew very close to the mountains; I thought that if could stick my hand out the window I could probably touch the snow. As the plane approached the runaway, it flew very close to a monastery, a beautiful white building decorated with red and gold ornaments and a huge statue of Buddha right in front. I thought that I would love to visit it if possible.

As soon as I set a foot out of the plane, I felt quite dizzy; the altitude really hit me hard, as Leh is more than 3.500 meters above sea level. My stomach turned upside down and the magic of being up in the Himalayas quickly vanished. As soon as I walked out the airport doors, I saw this man with a huge placard with my name written on it and an equally huge smile waiting for me.

"Namaste, Stanzin".

"Julley, Ms Gaby; we don't say Namaste here in Ladakh; here the main language is Ladakhi".

"Julley, Stanzin, this is for you from Dev". I handed him the rucksack and his eyes just lit up.

Stanzin was a rather short but muscular young man; his features were completely different to the Indian people in Delhi; he looked more like a Tibetan than a Hindu. We walked together to a small jeep.

"This is the best form of transport in the Himalayas; the roads are not often suitable for European cars", he said almost apologetic

"The jeep looks great".

"You don't look that great, Ms Gaby; I am sure it's altitude sickness. I am going to take you to a rather nice hotel of traditional ecological Ladakhi architecture called No Mind Retreat. You can stay there for 3 days until your body gets used to the altitude. There are beautiful mountain views and there you can join the meditation, yoga and vegetarian cooking classes, there is a very secluded monastery not far from the hotel, set out of the tourist route, very quiet and traditional".

"Sounds idyllic".

"It is, Dev loves that hotel and usually stays there all the time, he doesn't like travelling too much".

"Where are we going afterwards?"

"I am going to take you around Ladakh, ending up in Srinagar in Kashmir. After the 3 days of adjusting are over, we´ll come back to visit Leh. I will show you the Royal Palace, the former residence of the royal family of Ladakh, built in the same style and about the same time as the Potala Palace in Tibet. The majority of the population here we are Tibetan Buddhists and this region is known as little Tibet. You will see that when you go to the monastery: the monks wear the typical Tibetan robes. Most of them came from Tibet when they had to flee due to the Chinese invasion and they all settled around the Himalayas. As you probably know the Dalai Lama lives in Dharmsala, together with 10.000 other monks but there are lots of monasteries; we call them Gompas around this area; we can't visit them all but I will take you to visit some of them. I will take you around pretty remarkable places and will tell you all about them when we get there".

"That sounds absolutely amazing".

We reached a great big bamboo gate and then we entered an enclosed area where a huge statue of a happy Buddha was placed at the entrance welcoming the guests. There were a few chalet style bungalows, doted around the most lavishing gardens, full of fruit trees and flowers. I was led to one of the bungalows; it had very basic furniture with a fabulous window overlooking the mountains. What a view! Who needs furniture when you have those vistas right in front of you. After a short while, there was a knock at the door. It was Stanzin bringing a tray with some tea and biscuits.

"This a herbal tea, but a special herb to help you ease the altitude sickness and also a few biscuits made with special ingredients to help you with your upset stomach".

"How did you know my stomach is hurting?"

"Most visitors suffer the same when they just arrive here, and this will help. We use ayurvedic medicine here in this region; it's all made with roots and herbs".

"I would love to find out more about ayurvedic medicine".

"I can take you to an ayurvedic hospital one day if you want to; there is a very good one in Leh and they are not very expensive. The doctor will take your pulse and he will know immediately what is wrong with you and will give you the appropriate medicine".

"That would be great, thanks".

"Now, you better rest and enjoy the view, but make sure you drink lots of tea. I will come later with a miso soup unless you want to go to the restaurant and have a proper meal… although today I suggest you keep it light".

"A miso soup will be just fine, Stanzin, but can you give me the password for the internet please?"

"There is no internet here, Miss Gaby. You will have to wait until we get back to Leh; have a good rest".

I must have fallen sleep and was woken up by Stanzin knocking at the door again; it was completely dark and all I could see was millions of stars twinkling at a distance. I cannot recall ever seeing so many starts in the sky. Maybe in the Sahara dessert.

"Hello, Stanzin, come in".

"Julley, Julley. Miss Gaby, I'm just bringing you the miso soup. I came once before but you didn't open the door; you were probably asleep".

"Yes, I just woke up".

"That is good; keep resting and you will feel much better tomorrow".

"See you tomorrow".

I took the cup of miso soup and sat by the window, admiring the silhouette of the mountains against the backdrop of the starry sky.

I was woken up at the crack of down by the distant sound of a rooster and some sheep and I could also hear the faint sound of people singing. So peaceful! This was very relaxing and a far cry from the noisy Indian cities. I put something on and went out. I was starving; I walked across the lawn and met some guests doing yoga. I asked for the dining room and they pointed me to a large kiosk. I saw Stanzin sitting in a table with other people. He immediately stood up.

"Julley, Miss Gabby".

“Finish your breakfast, Stanzin”.

“I rather come and sit with you. How are you feeling this morning?”

“I’m feeling much better and very hungry”,

“Oh, good; that is a good sign. Still, you have to take it easy today. There is a morning meditation in an hour’s time in the main room and as you’ve just seen there is yoga and you can also go hiking, although is better to leave the hiking until tomorrow. You can walk around the hotel gardens today; is very peaceful here”.

“I heard some singing; where is that coming from?”

“It’s harvest season and all the villagers get together to gather the crops”.

“Can I go and watch?”

“Yes; we can go there after breakfast. It’s not too far but I want you to take it easy today. In the afternoon, I will drive you to the Likhir Gompa, that’s the monastery that’s close by, for the evening prayers. I am sure you will like that”.

After the most delicious breakfast, we started to walk across the fields. It felt crisp and fresh but not extremely cold, just like a nice sunny winter’s day in London. I had to walk slowly as I ran out of breath quite fast as if I had never done any exercise in years. Stanzin saw me struggling and laughed.

“I told you to take it easy. It takes 3 days for your body to adjust; I’ll go and get the jeep for the way back”.

I laughed back and felt like and old stupid lady. But when we finally reached the field that was being harvested, my efforts were rewarded with the most wonderful scene: all the villagers were working and singing, and the children playing nearby. I thought I had gone backwards in time. We sat on some large stones and I just stared at the whole scenery with the villagers singing and the mountains. I was transported to an old period film, but somehow this was real and happening in the XXI Century.

"All the crops are divided equally between them and any leftovers are taken to the Sunday market in Leh and the money is divided between them too", said Stanzin explaining me what was going on.

"God; why can't we all live like this; the world would definitely be a much better place".

"Most of the villages around here subsist like this; there is no crime and no competition, and it's a good way of life". We stayed there admiring the scene and after a while Stanzin looked at me and said:

"You wait here, Miss Gaby; I'll go and get the jeep".

For once in my life, I did not argue; I do not think I could have walked an inch more.

Back at the hotel I was sitting in a lounger enjoying the sun when one of the guests came toward me and handed me a tube of sunscreen.

"You better put some or otherwise you are going to get sunburnt; you have to be very careful at this altitude".

"Thanks, that is very kind of you; I'm Gaby".

"I'm Wagner; nice to meet you too. I haven't seen you before. When did you arrive?"

"I arrived yesterday but have spent most of the time sleeping".

"Don't worry; it will pass soon enough"

"Three days that's what everybody says; I travel around the globe only to spend my time in bed", I said laughing out loud.

"Back in Germany my doctor gave me some pills that are normally given to people that are going to climb Mount Everest and they did wonders for me; never felt sick at all".

"Do you have any spare ones?"

"Yes, I'll go and get you some".

A few minutes later Wagner came back with a jar of pills; he opened it up and gave me 3 pills. He was a tall blond guy, with blue deep eyes that looked a bit like Brad Pitt, not bad to see such a handsome man in the middle of the Himalayas.

"Take half a pill in the morning, and half in the evening during the next three days and you will be as good as new in no time, and after 3 days your body would have adjusted to the altitude so you won't need them anymore".

"Sounds wonderful", I said and I took my first half straight away.

"How long have you been here, Wagner?"

"Nearly a month".

"One month without internet?"

"That's been the best part; total bliss; I had become a slave of the senseless mobile and internet. I was a bank branch manager until I suffered an emotional breakdown. A friend suggested meditation and yoga classes and my teacher had just come back from this place and when she spoke about it I didn't think it about it twice: I booked a flight and here I am on my way to full recovery. I'm a totally different person and I attribute it partly to not having an internet connection".

"Wow, that's a great story!"

"It's not just my story; I'm sure many people around the world have fallen prey of the internet and they could benefit from totally disconnection. No doubt it has been a great invention; on the one hand it has made the world a smaller place, we can connect with someone in another corner of the world in seconds, it wasn't that long ago that to place a call it would take days and it would cost an arm and a leg. And on the other hand it has disconnected us from nature, from our friends and our loved ones. We spend too much time searching on the internet when the most important people, the ones that we should be paying attention to, are often right next to us and we totally ignore them just to look at that screen. When I first arrived, it was quite hard not having internet; I kept looking at my dead phone as if I had lost a close friend. But then I started to enjoy the view of this wonderful place, I started to really see the mountains and the sky and enjoy the smell of nature and that's when I started to feel better".

"When you go back you should give talks about it; I am sure that lots of people will benefit from it".

"I intend to; I could never go back to my old life. I will probably go and teach yoga and meditation and how to look after ourselves mentally and physically. Mental health is a very big issue in the world right now, and something that most of us are ashamed to talk about. When I was having my breakdown, I was the last one to admit it and I hurt the closest people to me, my marriage ended in divorce and I eventually lost my job".

"I am so sorry".

"Don't be; everything happens for a reason, and what's important now is what I do with my life from now on. And I intend to go back and help people before they hit rock bottom like I did".

"That's really making me think what I should do when I get back to London. I took a sabbatical after a middle age crisis and I have been travelling ever since in search of something that I seem to have lost along the way but I'm not quite sure what yet".

"Believe me, being here without internet and searching inside yourself will help you find the sparkle in life that you seem to have lost, but I am sure that's somewhere right here inside you", Wagner said touching my heart, and he seemed to have touched it not only physically but he touched me right inside my soul. At that point, I started to cry quite uncontrollably. Wagner gave me a big hug and Stanzin came running towards me.

"Are you okay, Miss Gaby?"

"Yes, Stanzin; just having a little cry but I am feeling much better now".

"Wagner, this is Stanzin, my guide and now my friend".

"Hello, Stanzin, pleased to meet you too".

"Miss Gaby, we have to leave now to the Likhir Gompa if you want to make it to the evening prayer".

"May I come with you? I usually walk up there but I won't make it in time today if I have to go on foot".

"Of course, please do, then you can show me what to do".

"Go and get a thick coat as it does get very cold once the sun goes down".

"I don't have any; I wasn't intending to come here when I left London".

"I'll lend you one for today, but Stanzin, make sure you take her to buy one in Leh and also buy a good sleeping bag as it's very cold in the hotels around here. They never seem to have enough blankets and hardly any of them have central heating".

"Wagner, you have already started your mission of looking after people mentally and physically right here with me. See you in the jeep in five minutes".

We started driving up the mountains and suddenly, after a bend, I could see this majestic Gompa and right in front a colossal statue of Maitreya regarded as the future Buddha; there was a big prayer wheel by the gate of the Gompa.

"I have to drop you here, Miss Gaby as I can't go any further in the jeep. Will you be okay walking?"

"I am feeling great, Stanzin. Wagner gave me some tablets and I feel I can run all the way to the top of Mount Everest without losing my breath".

"I'll be waiting in the cafeteria across the road".

We got off the jeep and Wagner went to the prayer wheel and started spinning the wheel while reciting the mantra Om mani padme hum,

"Come and join me. Let's walk around the prayer wheel repeating after me "Om mani padme hum", to collect good Karma and get rid of negativity".

"I could do with getting rid of lots of negativity. I better stay here all night".

"Let's go, you don't want to miss the prayer", Wagner said while tending me his hand. Just the thought of holding Brad Pitt's hand made me shiver and at least I knew he was already divorced. God, here I am going on to an evening prayer while praying for something else; when will I ever change? I could feel myself blushing. I just hoped he did not notice. We walked up the stairs to the huge golden statue, set on a highly decorated base, just behind it, but after another flight of stairs, we finally entered the Gompa, and God, was I glad for the tablets Wagner gave me! I do not think I would have managed without them. The sight when we entered the temple was amazing; it was mainly decorated in red and gold, and right in the middle behind a glass case were statues of Bodhisattva, Amitabha, three large statues of Sakyamuni, Maitreya and Tsong Khapa. Their names were clearly displayed at the front of each statue. And right in front were six rows of seats for the lamas and a throne for the Head Lama; there were also some beautiful paintings on the walls. Wagner indicated to me that we should seat at the back in a row of seats left for visitors. There were a few other people there and Wagner said hello to all of them, so I gathered they were all staying at the same hotel. A few minutes later the monks started to come in and took their places on the rows of benches; the ones at the front had some musical instruments, like bells and drums made of metal and quite ornate. The head lama said a few words in Tibetan and they soon started the chanting. It started very slow and then it got faster and faster and the energy of the place became electrifying. I had never heard or seen anything like it; it sounded like the humming of thousands of bees. I closed my eyes and just felt my heart pounding and started to sweat. The whole chanting session must have lasted about an hour; when it finally stopped, the monks stood up and quietly left, and we also stood up and started walking towards the main gate. As soon as I set a foot outside the door I was hit by a strong cold wind. Now I knew what Wagner meant by a bit cold, it was freezing! We all ran towards the cafeteria where Stanzin was waiting for us, together with a minibus driver from the hotel. Wagner introduced me and we all went straight to the bus and my jeep. When we arrived, we went to the dining kiosk, where a huge spread of food was waiting for us. It was all very delicious and I was very surprised not to see a curry dish; it was more like the Chinese food we eat back in London, consisting of dumplings, noodles and lots of vegetables, all grown in the hotel's vegetable garden. It was lovely to meet and exchange stories with the other guest; it was a good friendly atmosphere. No mobiles, just laughter. When the time came to say goodbye, they all said.

"See you at 5am, Gaby"

"See you at 5am for what?"

"The morning prayer is at 6am but we all walk to the Gompa together, and the minibus will pick up us afterwards so we can make it back in time for breakfast; it's lovely seeing the sunrise between the mountains. I'll come and knock at your door" said Wagner

"No need for makeup", said one of the girls in the group.

"You'll probably need to break the door; I don't think I have ever woken up so early".

"That's the spirit; see you tomorrow"

I went back to my room and got my clothes ready for the next day; I stayed watching the stars for a while and before I knew, all I could hear was Wagner at the door; it was already 5am and it was still pitch black. I put my clothes on and went out.

"I must be mad to be doing this".

"I thought you were a fearless woman travelling by yourself in India and here you are crying like a baby just because it's 5am and you are walking up to heaven".

I gave him a big smile and when we came out into the main gate at the hotel, the rest of the gang was waiting there and they all clapped.

"We thought you weren't coming".

"Wagner did blow the door down".

Hahaha!

One of the girls came quite close to me and whispered in my ear:

"I thought he was going to stay with you; the way that you were looking at each other last night".

I laughed and just kept on walking. Was it that obvious? I thought to myself. Maybe tonight, although I was leaving in two days; so what was the point? I was exhausted by the time we reached the monastery, medicine or not, it was quite a steep climb. The only thing that kept me going was the view of the mountains through the faint light of dawn and Wagner's arm wrapped around my waist pushing me forward. We all sat in the same back bench as the previous evening and the monks all started to come out and took their places in the front benches, but this time they were accompanied by lots of very young boys all dressed in red gowns. The head lama also talked for quite a lot longer in his deep slow voice and then the chanting began, and it sounded even lovelier with the voices of the children also joining. When it all finished, we started walking towards the minibus, and some of the children came running through. As if reading my mind Wagner said.

"There is a school attached to the monastery. It's quite an honour for a family to have a child chosen to come and study here and then they will become lamas' themselves".

"So, they have no option?"

"I don't think so".

"Julley, Julley", they all shouted

"They look so cute in their tiny robes".

"And at least here they will have good food and a good education".

"But they must miss their families; some of them are so young".

"I suppose they do, but it's a tradition and they all seem happy".

The minibus was waiting for us and we all boarded it and went to have our breakfast. Stanzin was waiting for me, quite worried as he thought I was overdoing it, but happy that I was enjoying myself.

"I promise I will take it easy all day and you can drive me to the Gompa this afternoon as I don't think I can walk up there again in one day", I said.

"Okay. I'll come looking for you just before 5pm".

"Great, thanks".

I went to the garden and laid on the grass, and a few minutes later Wagner came and sat next to me.

"Do you mind if I join you?"

"Of course not; I am just tired and I don't think I can move a finger, so don't ask me to do yoga or anything strenuous".

"Will talking do?"

I just smiled

"But this time, you have to do the talking; the other day I went on and on about me and the internet connection and didn't let you talk. Tell me about your middle life crisis?", said Wagner staring directly into my eyes.

"I was doing all the idiotic things to try and stay young and to fill that gap I have somewhere inside me. I set out in search of that something and as I am now realizing that something can't be found in the outside world and only I can search within me to find that peace and quiet we all want. Just as the monks do, but then, I do not want to become a nun to do so. I do not want to live in a monastery in order to achieve it; there must be a balance between both worlds and that is what I am aiming for. I believe we come to this earth to enjoy everything that life has to offer, food, nature, sun, rain, friends, work parties, sex, but not just doing things unconsciously but really feeling and appreciating everything, never forgetting that we are spiritual beings having an earth experience. That's why life for me locked in a monastery is not the answer". I gave a big sight as if I had just said something that was good for me to be getting out of my chest.

"That's also why I believe that internet is making us loose that connection with earth, nature, life. And in my personal life, losing that connection made me lose my mind; but I understand it better and I am ready to go back and find that balance".

"You just hit the nail with the hammer: Finding Balance, that is the key to a good and healthy life", I said realizing how important that was, just as Dev Patel have found in Pushkar.

"Internet in not all bad, but the main issue is finding the balance between using it and not overdoing it. And so is everything else in life; we can only enjoy so much food but as soon as we overdo it, we get sick. Same with relationships; if we don't give each other breathing space we get bored with the other person. So balance, balance, balance and it's easier to say it than to find it". As soon as he said that, Stanzin appeared walking towards us.

"Hello, Stanzin; will be ready in a minute; see you in the car park".

"We'll have to keep talking about finding balance later on; I think it's really interesting. I only have one day left here; I'm going early in the morning the day after tomorrow".

"I will be sorry to see you go", he said looking at me with a sad expression and offered me his hand to help me get up.

We went up to the Likir Gompa and sitting down to meditate I thought it was important to really go within to find my inner peace; if I was going to find a balance in my life, it was important that I would fully meditate when it was time to do so. That evening with the chanting of the monks, I was transported to a magical space and I started to feel really at ease with myself.

I did not feel hungry when I got back to the hotel; I just had a miso soup to warm up and went back to my room. I could feel Wagner's eyes looking at me.

"I will come by at 5am".

"I'll be ready", I said, waving to everyone. Back in my room I was feeling a bit melancholic; part of me wished he had followed me to my room and the other half just wanted to be alone… finding that balance was more difficult than I expected.

It was lovely to see Wagner's face standing by the door waiting for me first thing in the morning. The walking seemed easier; at least I was finding a balance between health and pray. Now it was just love and work I had to somehow manage. And back in London to juggle everything was going to be an uphill struggle. The morning prayer was my favourite; I was charged after the night's rest and seeing the children praying with such devotion was very rewarding.

After breakfast, Wagner asked me if he could talk to me. It was a very cold morning so I asked him if he wanted to come to my room and we could talk while he watched me pack. I had asked in the hotel if they could wash my clothes so I could take everything clean for my journey to Srinagar. I put my luggage on top of the bed and I started packing under Wagner's watchful eye.

"I have quite a few things I have been buying along the way; mainly presents for my friends back in London", I said to Wagner, trying to justify myself for all the things I had to pack.

"Leave a bit of space for all the things you are going to go crazy for in Leh; the shops there are full of custom jewellery and beautiful cashmere scarfs that you won't find anywhere else".

"OMG, what on earth am I going to do with more temptations? I am not only running out of space but out of funds too".

Wagner burst out laughing

"Women will always find money and space in their luggage for a few more temptations. But there is one place in Leh that you should go and visit: the Tibetan Buddhist Monastery of Hemis, located about 40 kilometres from Leh. Stanzin should know where it is; that's the monastery that a Russian scholar named Nicolas Notovitch claims Jesus spent his lost years. He wrote a book, The Unknown Life of Christ, where he tells the story that at one point during his travels around Afghanistan and India he broke a leg and had to spend some time recovering in the Hemis Gompa. While there the monks showed him large volumes written in Tibetan telling the story of a child named Jesus born to a poor family in Israel. Jesus was referred to as the son of God in the texts that Notovitch translated. During his time at the monastery, one lama explained to Notovitch the full scope and extreme level of enlightenment that Jesus had reached. And also, if you believe the stories that Jesus survived the crucifixion, when you get to Srinagar make sure you visit an old building known as the Rozabal shrine, that is believed by some to be the real tomb of Jesus".

"Wow; that sounds amazing; for sure I will go; I remember watching the film The Da Vinci Code, where they mention that, but I didn't know it was actually here. There are no coincidences in life and me talking to you about it right now is not a coincidence".

"Thanks for that. I started my sabbatical journey walking the Camino in Spain and I am finishing this journey with another pilgrimage around India; there must be a connection and a deeper meaning to all this".

"I wish I could come with you but I now feel that my time in India must come to an end and I am ready to return to Dusseldorf. However, I was going to ask you for a lift to Leh; we could spend a couple of days there before you continue with your travels and I can make arrangements to fly back home".

"That would be marvellous; we can spend some time together and you can show me the Gompa", I said. At that point I could see Wagner's face brighten up. He stood up, placed my luggage on the floor and gently pushed me towards the bed. He kissed me and started to undress me. I was shaking like a teenage girl; and when Wagner took his jeans off, I was transported to the film Thelma and Louise when Brad Pitt seduced Geena Davies. We made love just as passionately as they did, having the Himalayan Mountains as the backdrop stage. Afterwards, we stayed in bed gazing at the mountains for a long time.

"I wanted to do this from the very first time I set my eyes on you; the suntan lotion was the only excuse I could find". We smiled at each other. "But I better go now, as I have to do my packing and inform the hotel I'm leaving and I don't want to miss our last trip to the Gompa", Wagner said as he stood up.

"See you at 5pm in the car park".

I stayed in my room and finished packing. I wished I had my mobile and could tell Linda all about this place and Wagner, but on the other hand, I was starting to feel the benefits of not having my mobile with me all the time. Balance, balance, balance. I went to meet Stanzin and I saw Wagner standing next to him in the car park.

"I'm already packed and ready to go".

"I'm happy if you are happy, Miss Gaby", said Stanzin, winking at me.

"Let's go up to the Gompa for the very last time; I am going to miss it. It's been one of the best experiences in my life and who knows, maybe I will come back one day", said Wagner with a lump in his throat.

On the way up, we were all just admiring the view as we got closer and closer to the Gompa. Wagner went straight to the school and took some sweets and some of his old jumpers for the children. We then sat at our usual place inside the temple; all eyes from the rest of the hotel gang were on us. The monks came in and the whole atmosphere was electrifying; when we finished Wagner went to thank the head lama and I could see tears rolling down his cheeks. I could only imagine how much this place meant to him; it had been his sanctuary and healing place during a very dark chapter in his life.

Back at the hotel, we had a very lovely farewell dinner party. We had music, we danced and sang and it was just a wonderful way of ending a lovely stay in this wonderful place.

Early next morning Wagner and I woke up to say goodbye to the gang on their way to the Gompa; we had breakfast with Stanzin and then we drove to Leh. On the way there I could see how beautiful the landscape was, dotted with stupas and crumbling mud-brick houses. When I arrived from Delhi it was already dark and I was feeling rather nauseous so didn't really appreciate it, but now I was feeling full of life and in great company. What a difference the last 3 days had made to my life! And all without internet connection: all down to a good balance between, food, love and meditation. I felt whole. We started to discuss what we were going to do in Leh. Stanzin said he would take me to the Hemis Gompa on our way to the Nubra valley, where we were going after Leh, as it was on its way.

"When we arrive, we can go to check-in at the hotel and then you can go and wonder around the town and I can go and book you an appointment at the Ayurveda hospital for the day after tomorrow", said Stanzin.

"I would love to go there too", said Wagner; "I've been meaning to go since I arrived and have never managed to do so. I also have to find a travel agency so I can book a flight back to Germany".

"That's settled for tomorrow. First the hospital and afterwards we can visit the Palace, Stanzin".

We arrived at a nice hotel set in the footsteps of the mountains just on the outskirts of Leh. We were given a lovely room overlooking the town and the palace, and there was internet connection, so Wagner booked his flights online. He was travelling to Delhi and taking a connecting flight to Dusseldorf later on the same day.

"I never thought this day would come, when I would gather the courage to go back to Germany. And meeting you have given me the strength to do so; I am very grateful".

"But I didn't do anything".

"You made me realize I was ready". He looked at me with loving eyes and held my hand.

"I would love to stay in this bed with you all day, but I really want to walk around Leh and see what goodies I can find; besides, I need to buy a coat and a sleeping bag".

"No need for that you can keep my coat and I don't need my sleeping bag anymore".

"Are you sure? This coat looks expensive".

"Something to remember me by".

I gave him a big kiss, put my coat on and went out. We walked through narrow alleys lined with mud-brick Ladakhi houses until we reached the centre of town. Leh was surprisingly crowded, full of tourist gearing up to start their trekking experience. Wagner explained to me that Leh was a favourite starting point for people that were trekking the Himalayas, not only by foot but also on motorbikes. He looked at me with loving eyes and told me there was a big mixture of people walking between the Ladakhi's and the odd monk; it was a very colourful place. The streets were lined with shops selling just about everything you can think of: clothes, jewellery, food, kitchen utensils and Buddha figurines of any size. My eyes could not quite take it all. I did succumb to a few temptations and helped Wagner buy a few presents to take back home to his family and friends; it was a very enjoyable afternoon. In the evening we went back to the hotel and had a wonderful dinner with Stanzin. Afterwards, we went back to our room and made love until we fell asleep. I woke up early; I kept looking at my mobile, but could not turn it on. I knew if I did, I would find many messages and just did not want to deal with them just yet.

After breakfast, we went to the Ayurvedic hospital. I was quite surprised to find it was so big; it was just like any normal western hospital, a spacious white building including A&E and ambulances. I was expecting a small obscure house in the middle of nowhere.

"About 80% of the population here in India use Ayurvedic medicine or a combination of both western and Ayurvedic; it's highly regarded and therefore there is no difference in the treatment of both", said Stanzin, probably realizing my mouth was wide open when I saw the large hospital complex.

We walked into a large waiting area jam-packed with rows of benches with hardly any places left to sit down. Luckily, we didn't have to wait long before I was called in to a consultation room, where a female doctor was waiting for me; she was wearing a white gown on top of a sari and bearing a small dot on her forehead between her eyebrows. The mark is known as a bindi, traditionally worn by women for religious purposes or to indicate that they are married.

"Namaste", she said bowing her head. "What brings you here today?"

"To be honest I am not sure; I can't say what is wrong with me other that I keep feeling I have something missing in my life".

"Westerners, you come here to India searching for a guru to fix your life thinking that there is something missing when we are already whole", she said smiling at me as she grabbed a hold of my wrist.

"Let me see if there is anything really wrong with you for me to sort out, but that longing you have inside, can't be fixed by me or any guru; only you can heal your soul. There is no medicine that can cure that yearning inside you". She took my pulse and started writing a few things in a notebook.

"I'm going to give you some herbal medicine for anxiety and I also recommend that you buy Shilajit. It's an effective and safe supplement that can have a positive effect on your overall health and well-being; it's a natural substance found here in the Himalayan mountains and we commonly use it in Ayurvedic medicine as it's rich in fulvic acid and minerals, very good for immunity, memory and energy. It will also help with your joint pains and has anti-ageing properties".

"OMG, what is the name of it? I will probably need to take a bag full back home with me".

"SHILAJIT; I will write it down for you and no need to buy a big bag full of it; you only need to dissolve a very small amount in lukewarm water; the taste is not very pleasant but it's a wonderful supplement".

I thanked her, left, and asked Wagner to go in. He spent quite a long time inside the consultation room and I just wondered what was wrong with him; I hoped it was not serious. He came out looking quite sombre and with a very long list of medicines to buy. We went to the pharmacy; the medicines looked identical: small back pellets, which were put into small bags with their labels written in Hindi and luckily also in English. I also asked for the Shilajit and was given a small bag with a black paste inside it that smelt and looked like tar. Stanzin asked me not to buy the Shilajit here as we were going to one of the places in the mountains where they made it and it would probably be of a better quality and cheaper. I bought a small amount anyway, as I wanted to start taking it straight away. Wagner was very quiet and when I asked him about what the doctor had said, he did not really want to talk about it, so I just changed the subject, as I did not want him to feel uncomfortable.

We went to the palace, but could not see much as it was under restoration due to its dilapidated state, but at least in the palace museum there was a rich collection of jewellery, ornaments, ceremonial dresses and crowns and Tibetan paintings. I just wondered how such a beautiful palace had been left to deteriorate so much. Stanzin drove us back to the town centre and he asked if he could use the rest of the day to visit some friends. We just asked him to drop us off at a good restaurant and told him that we would spend the rest of the afternoon wondering around the street markets.

Wagner was still very quiet and hardly touched his food; I asked what was wrong and he said nothing; he just said he would rather spend the last afternoon with me in the hotel than walking around buying things he did not really need. Back in our room, he finally started talking about how he was feeling.

"Sorry, I haven't been myself today; talking to the doctor brought back memories of my depression and left me feeling as if I could have done spending more time here. She said that it did not matter how much exercise I did, how many supplements I took, how well I feed myself, but that as long as I did not heal my mind, illnesses would always creep up, time and time again.

"I want to go back home and start again and put into practice everything that I learnt here", he continued saying after a pause. "I dream of setting up a school to teach people how to look after their mind, Body & Spirit, but how can I teach others if I am not sure I am capable of looking after myself?"

"Wagner, you are a wonderful man and since I've met you; all you have been doing is looking after me; that is something embodied in you. Your depression was probably a lesson you had to overcome so that you can really understand the people you will help to heal. Life has its own way of teaching us things and in our darkest moments, we learn our most valuable lessons. I think the doctor made a good point that would be important for that future school of yours: that it's just as important for people to heal their minds so they can heal their body and souls".

He looked at me and held my face with his hands.

"You have such a wonderful way to make me see and understand things; I feel as if I have known you all my life and yet it has been only a few days. I am really going to miss you".

"I am going to miss you too, but that's when internet connection comes in handy; we can stay in touch and I am sure we will meet again pretty soon".

"Talking about internet connections, I've noticed you haven't turned your mobile on".

"I want to do this Himalayan experience without the interference from the outside world; one email can change the way I feel that day, a problem will send me into a worrying frenzy and there is nothing I can do from here, so anything pending will have to wait until I get back to London".

"So, I won't hear from you until you get back to London?"

"I am afraid not, so better make the most of it today". And I jumped on top of him and started to undress him.

It was a bitterly cold morning when we woke up; there was no time for lazing around as Wagner had an early flight to catch and Stanzin and me were off to my Himalayan adventure. Wagner had booked a taxi as the airport was in the opposite direction to where I was going, but deep down I think he did not want me to go to the airport. He gave me a big hug.

"This is not a good bye, this is just a see you soon, Gaby", he said with a big lump in his throat.

"See you soon, Wagner; it's been an absolute pleasure, a gift from life". I quickly turned round as I did not what him to see me shed a tear.

"Good bye, Stanzin, look after her for me". He waved at Stanzin as he got into his cab.

I got into the jeep and we set off.

"Stanzin, let´s go and find the Srinagar highway".

"This is it, Miss Gaby, and this is the best part of it".

It was only a small road with hardly any markings and this was supposed to be their highway; no wonder Stanzin drove a jeep to travel around; we also had to steer through flocks of sheep, road accidents, police stoppages and being a single lane road made it very difficult to overtake other vehicles. But the view of the mountains and stupas covered with prayer flags was breathtaking; everyone just shouted "Julley, Julley", as we drove by. It took us more than three hours to reach the Hemis Gompa and when we arrived, the place was full of people dancing and the whole sight was amazing.

"We have just arrived in the middle of the Hemis Festival; here they celebrate every year the birth anniversary of Guru Padamsambhav. It is a two-day celebration, which marks the victory of good over evil. Legend has it that Lord Padamsambhav defeated the dark forces and therefore the people of Ladakh celebrate the day of his birth with this huge festival", said Stanzin very enthusiastically.

"Can we stay here? I would love to see it all".

"It's difficult to find accommodation during the festival; as you can see it's very crowded but I have friends here and I can ask them if we can stay with them. That's if you don't mind; home stays are very popular in Ladakh; you can see how people live here and they welcome the extra income. You wait for me here; we can meet by the souvenir stalls in an hour".

"That sounds great. See you later".

I started mingling amongst the crowd; there were many tourists but mainly local people all dressed in their best traditional attires. Everyone seemed really happy, the sound of the music playing and the vast sea of colour was one of the most vibrant events I had ever come across. I wondered if Jesus had indeed lived here during his lost years if he had witnessed this festival. I wished he had and I hoped he had enjoyed himself too.

I walked towards the stalls full of Tibetan souvenirs. Oh, Dear, more temptations! But my priority was to try and find Stanzin as I did not want to get lost in this place. I started to panic a bit but just by the first stall, I saw Stanzin waiting for me.

"Julley, Miss Gaby. All sorted. I will introduce you to my friends later on because right now we must hurry as the best event is starting in a minute: the masked dance performance called Cham. It is a slow dance portraying the war between good and evil whe-re the good ones win!" We found a good spot where to watch the dance. The whole event with the music playing, the colourful mask costumes and having the monastery as backdrop was jaw dropping.

"Who are the dancers?"

"The Lamas".

"Hahahaha, can you imagine our priests dressing up and dancing like that? NEVER!", I said it out laud and a few of the tourist turned round and laughed too. I thought of Wagner; I was sure he would have loved to be here, maybe I should have asked him to travel with me, but then it was too late, he was proba-bly flying now on his way back to Germany.

After the dance, Stanzin showed me inside the monastery; it was very beautiful and also very quiet; there were no evening prayers as the lamas were all in the festival, so there wouldn't be an opportunity for me to ask any of them about the manuscripts and the period that Jesus supposedly spent in this place. I asked Stanzin and he said he had heard the rumours and that most tourists came asking the same question but that he had no idea. I just sat quietly at the back on the main temple, closed my eyes and meditated, trying to visualize Jesus being there with me and I was soon engulfed by a very happy energy. I believe that if Jesus had indeed spent time in the Hemis Gompa, it must have been one of the happiest periods in his life.

Stanzin started to look out for his friends; it was very difficult to find anyone amongst the crowded monastery courtyard, but eventually he found them and I was introduced to them. They were all gorgeously dressed and their two beautiful young daughters looked like porcelain dolls. We all walked back to their house, a typical Ladakhi mud house; inside it was all covered with rugs and there was a wood burner that gave a cosy warm atmosphere to the whole place. Stanzin showed me to my room; he had placed my bag and sleeping bag on top of the bed and then he showed me the bathroom……well, better don't even mention it, but at least it was clean. Seeing my discomfort Stanzin just said looking towards the hole in the ground:

"Sorry, but our toilets are all like this".

"Don't worry, Stanzin, I'll be okay; it's not the first time I've used one of these".

The woman of the house had prepared dumpling soup and some vegetable noodles, all very delicious. I could not say much as besides Stanzin nobody else could speak English., I just smiled and said thank you. I went to my room that was absolutely freezing; I was so glad that Wagner had left me his sleeping bag; I snuggled inside it and I could almost feel him right there with me.

I woke up to the delicious smell of food; I quickly dressed up and went to the main room where the whole family was having breakfast. I sat down at the table and was given the most delicious chai tea I have ever tasted and some home-made bread. Afterwards we said goodbye; I gave them all a big hug and Stanzin and me continued our journey towards the Nubra Valley. We started climbing towards the Khardungla pass, one of the highest passes in the world at more than 5.300 meters. The road there was treacherous, with many landslides, forcing Stanzin to drive right by the edge of a huge precipice that made my stomach cringe. Definitely not for the faint hearted! But the views! Sorry if I keep mentioning it, but I can't even describe it. I saw yacks for the first time ever in my life; I got off the jeep to take some pictures and was surprised at how docile they were. I even managed to stroke them. I also saw many monasteries doted around the highest mountains; I wanted to visit them all but Stanzin said that most of them do not even have road access. The pass itself was bitterly cold and it was snowing; I wanted to take a picture next to the landmark showing the altitude and found it very difficult to breath. I was gasping for air and really struggled to walk the few meters from the jeep. When I finally stood next to the landmark, I felt that I was on top of the world and just imagined what people must feel when they conquer the summit of one of the eight-thousanders.

The descent towards the Nubra Valley was just as treacherous but as we got closer to the valley, the roads improved and we managed to drive a bit faster, enjoying the warmer weather and the sight of the sand and dunes in the middle of the Himalayas. The valley is a high altitude cold desert, but just before we reached our destination, we stopped at the Diskit Gompa, the largest Buddhist monastery in the Nubra Valley set imbedded in the rocks in the foot of the mountains with a very large Buddha statue right in front. I slowly climbed towards the main temple while Stanzin waited for me by the jeep. I arrived just as two monks were starting the evening prayer; there were no places at the back of the temple to sit down and meditate, but one of the monks saw me trying to find a space and he gestured for me to sit next to them. I sat close to them but very careful not to touch them; they started a slow chant with a very deep voice and then gradually gained speed; one of them was passing the pages of a small book, while the other was ringing the Tibetan Tingsha bells. I soon found myself immersed in the energy of the chanting and being so close to the monks meant that I was really a part of it and it transported me into an alter state. It was overwhelming and I started to shake and sweat and when I thought I could not take it anymore the chanting stopped. The monks stood up, bowed and left. I remained there for a few minutes gaining back my composure and thought that maybe the monks had just allowed me to take a glimpse into their world. Back in the jeep, I told Stanzin about it, and he said it was a very rare from the monks, especially as I was a woman. We drove up to the village of Hunter. Stanzin said we couldn't go any further as tourists were not allowed beyond this point; he found us a nice place to stay, in a large white house set in the middle of a eucalyptus tree forest that smelt wonderful. The house had been converted into a small hotel and after I had dinner I went to my room, and there on the bedside table was a big sign "internet access code 5577", a temptation I could not resist anymore. I quickly took my mobile out of my bag and turned it on. As soon as I placed the access code, it started to go crazy, bleeping nonstop. Half of the messages were from Linda; she was very worried and also wanted me to know what to do with my flat as my tenants were moving out soon.

"Dear Linda, I'm still alive and quacking; I'm in the middle of the Himalayas, where in most places they haven't even heard about internet. I have a wonderful local guide that is driving me around these beautiful mountains, and no, before you even think about it, he is not my lover, although I did meet a wonderful German guy that unfortunately had to leave two days ago: he really took my breath away, he might be the one. In regards to the flat, please call my cleaner and have her thoroughly clean everything. I will be going back to London in a couple of weeks. I will let you know as soon as I buy my return ticket. As to the office, please don't even mention it; I don't want to think what I am going to do with my job just yet. I might end up living in Germany, who knows. Miss you lots, can't wait to get back and tell you all about my adventures, love Gaby".

I saw messages from George, Richard, Yousef, Sophia, Anika and I few more but I just left them there;

I would reply to everyone once I was back in London. I deleted all the rubbish and kept searching to see if I had missed one from Wagner; but no; he had not written anything yet.

I went out of my room and stepped on the courtyard. I never got tired of admiring the stars from this altitude; they seemed so close that you could almost touch them. There were a few people on the courtyard, all glued to their mobiles, probably having only managed to connect for the first time in a few days, same as me. But it was not a pretty sight; I preferred the atmosphere in the hotel in Likhir, where everyone talked to each other, but here they were all immersed in their own world. I went back to my room as I was pretty tired; as I tried to sleep, I couldn't stop thinking of the experience at the monastery; the meditation with the monks had been very special and I wished I could learn to get to those alter states on my own.

I was woken up by the loud noise of birds in the woodland; it was another crisp cold morning. I went to find Stanzin at the breakfast.

"Julley, Miss Gaby, did you sleep well?"

"Yes, thank you Stanzin. What are we doing today?"

"You are going to cross the dessert in a two hump Bactrian camel. You can take a swimming costume if you want as you are going to cross a hot spring and I will be waiting for you in Diskit and after lunch we can go at visit the Alchi Gompa and sleep on the foothills of the Lamayuru Gompa".

"That sounds like a lot for one day; can we skip the dessert crossing? I have just been to the Sahara and don't really fancy doing that again".

"As you wish, Miss Gaby, but I brought you here so you can see this dessert; at least let me walk you to the edge and we can have a short stroll around the dunes".

"That sounds perfect".

We walked along the eucalyptus forest until we reached the dessert. It was a light grey sand desert not like the red dunes of the Sahara, but nonetheless it was lovely. I walked up to the top of the hill of the closest large dune and just sat there admiring the view. I closed my eyes and did a short meditation and thought about Yousef and the magical evening I spent with him. Why couldn't I commit to just one guy? Why did I find that so difficult? Perhaps as some people enjoy living as a couple, get married and have children, some people are gay, maybe there are lots of people like me on this planet that just enjoy being alone, and appreciate the company of someone when it happens to appear. I did love being by myself. I enjoy my own company and I never feel lonely. I am happiest as how I am right now, just being here enjoying everything around me and taking it all in. My face lit up; just realizing that made me feel felt really happy. We are all different and maybe it was time I started to accept myself just as I was.

I walked back to the jeep and we set ourselves toward Alchi; we were once again on the very treacherous "highway" full of landslides and precipices. This time I hardly got of the jeep; I just wanted to reach the Alchi Gompa. I got really dizzy and unwell during the journey, so I asked Stanzin to try and find a place to stay in Alchi and I would go and visit both monasteries the following day. He found a room for me to stay in the Alchi Resort, a rather upmarket hotel and I welcomed the extravagance of central heating and a luxury bathroom with shower. I remained under the warm shower for at least half an hour and later on I walked around the grounds of the hotel. It was set amongst beautiful gardens, there were a few white and red buildings scattered around that housed two rooms on each building. I went to the mediation room and stayed there for a while before going to the dining room; at least people were talking to each other and I spotted a group of American tourists in a large table. I asked them if I could join them so we could exchange experiences. The main subject were the roads and how nerve racking and dangerous they were. They told me that the Khardungla pass had the highest death toll of any road in the world. I was just glad I had not added up to the statistics, but was not surprised given the number of accidents we had encountered during our journey. The Americans were going to the monastery the following day and they asked me if I wanted to join them. I said yes, and told Stanzin that he could have the morning off, that we could meet for lunch and could go to the Lamayuru Gompa in the afternoon.

"I like this hotel Stanzin, and I would like to stay here another night before we continue our journey to Srinagar".

"As you wish, Miss Gaby. I will meet you here for lunch tomorrow".

Early morning the following day I was going to Alchi in a bus full of Americans. As soon as I sat down, I started to regret it; I forgot how loud they could be and they all talked at the same time.

"May I seat next to you?, said a middle aged, tall, elegant woman, dressed in chequered trousers and a white blouse; she reminded me of Doris Day.

"Yes, please, be my guest"

"I adore your British accent. Why haven't I seen you in the tour before?"

"I just joined you for the visit to the monastery this morning; I am staying at the resort".

"What a shame you are not travelling with us; I could do with some decent company. I am a bit bored with these old age pensioners that are not in the least interested in the Buddhist traditions".

"I thought I had made a big mistake when I boarded the bus, but you know what they say; there are no coincidences in life and maybe we were meant to be together today", I said giving her a big smile.

A guide stood at the front of the bus and started talking.

"Good morning, campers; hope you had a good evening in this beautiful resort. We are now going to visit the Alchi Monastery, one of the oldest in Ladakh and unlike the other monasteries, Alchi is situated on lowland, not on a hilltop. Inside, the monastery houses thousands of rare and unique sculptures and paintings that go back to 11th century Western Tibet".

"It's good that they tell you all about a place before you visit it; my guide doesn't know much of the history of the places we are visiting. By the way I'm Gaby".

"I am Diana, like your Lady Di, and I bet I won't remember any of the stories when the tour ends".

"Memories are the best; I remember the people I meet and the places I visit".

We arrived at the monastery and there was another guide waiting for us by the entrance and as he started narrating by heart the story of the Monastery, I quickly moved towards the main temple. Diana came with me; we entered the shrine; its shape was different, it looked more like a museum and there were no monks around, only lots of tourist and no atmosphere to do any meditation. We walked back into the courtyard and it was full of souvenirs' stalls.

"This was not what I had been expecting. I wanted to find a quiet place of worship".

"Most of the monasteries we have visited with the excursion have been like this one; very much geared for the tourist industry".

"I am puzzled, as up until now I have only visited very quiet monasteries, except for Hemis, but that was due to the festival".

"That's because you are not travelling in a tour".

That is when I realized how special had been travelling with Stanzin; I could not wait to go back and thank him.

Stanzin was waiting for me in the dining room,

"Julley, Miss Gaby. How was Alchi Gompa?"

"Couldn't wait to get out of there. Too many tourists; why did you want me to see it in the first place?"

"I just wanted you to see the oldest gompa, but we were supposed to go to Lamayuru. That's a good gompa for meditation; we were going to stay in a small guesthouse next to it so you could walk for the evening and morning prayer".

"From now on I will only listen to you. We better go to Lamayuru after lunch and stay there tonight. I don't want to miss the afternoon prayer".

Diana looked at me with begging eyes, but we were travelling in opposite directions. But Stanzin, as if guessing that she wanted to go with us, stepped in:

"If she wants to come with us tonight, I will bring her back early in the morning before her bus leaves and while you are in your morning prayer".

"Yes, please", Diana said, clapping her hands. "I would love to join in you for the evening prayer".

Lamayuru was not too far from Alchi; we dropped our bags at the guesthouse and walked to the gompa; there was a prayer wheel by the entrance and walking around it and there was a monk there too but he was limping. I gestured in case he needed some help, but he replied in perfect English.

"I'm okay; thank you"

"You come from America?" said Diana recognizing his accent.

"I live in LA, but I was born here; I returned because I need some treatment in my leg and this is the best place to receive healing. Let's go inside; the prayer is starting soon".

We entered the Gompa and the monk started to tell us all about it.

"Lamayuru Gompa means the Eternal Monastery; it´s one of the largest and also one of the oldest; it has around 150 resident monks. He guided us around the temples showing us everything and explaining everything, especially about the lovely paintings on the walls. He talked with passion and it came from his heart. We arrived at the main temple and he asked us to seat by the side, quite close to where the head lama stool was; he sat directly in front of it. Soon after, many lamas started to come into the temple. They started filling up, row after row, until the temple was completely full. The head lama started the prayer in the usual deep voice and the monks answered back; he placed his hands in front of our monk friend and all the monks in the front started ringing Tibetan bells. It was the most wonderful captivating atmosphere. I looked at Diana and she was crying inconsolably; I held her hand and could feel that she was also shaking. The ceremony lasted around an hour; once it finished, we walked towards the main entrance where the American monk was waiting for us.

"Namaste, ladies; I'm sure you received lots of healing tonight; it was a very special ceremony for me, but I am sure you were meant to be here as well; go in peace".

"Namaste", we both replied to the monk, as we bowed and left.

We walked holding on to each other, making sure we did not fall down on the narrow footpath; it was very dark and bitterly cold. When we arrived back at the guesthouse, Stanzin was waiting with warm bowls of miso soup. Diana ran towards him and gave him a big hug.

"Thank you for making this possible for me; I came to the Himalayas just to experience this; it's something I will never forget", she said.

"Julley, Miss Diana; but you have Miss Gaby to thank; if she had not made me stop at Alchi yesterday you wouldn't be here with us tonight".

"Come on; let's eat, I am starving", I said to both of them.

We sat and ate a delicious vegetarian meal; the owner of the guesthouse came and sat with us and explained everything he had cooked for us.

"This is so much better than the cold food buffet we have to eat every day; I wished I had met you before and I could go with you but I have already paid for the whole tour".

"You can come next year and I can drive you around; I know the best gompas. You can ask Miss Gaby".

"I would like that very much, Stanzin; give me your details and I will surely come back here again".

I went back to my room and thought about how everything had worked out for the best. Life is so easy when we just go with the flow, but when we start over thinking and fight against the tide, that is when life becomes a struggle.

The following morning, we hugged and said goodbye; I went back to the gompa and she went back to the resort. There were not as many monks in the temple as the previous evening but it was a lovely prayer. I looked for our friend but didn't see him. I went back to the hostel and saw Stanzin already there waiting for me.

"Julley, Miss Gaby, when I left Miss Diana, she gave me a big tip. I didn't want her to pay me, but she wouldn't take no for an answer".

"Enjoy it, Stanzin, I am sure if she gave you the money, she thought you were worthy of it and she can probably afford it, so don't worry about it. Where are we going today?"

"We are going to see some rock paintings and then I am going to take you to the place where they make the Shilajit and also the best apricot oil in the Himalayas".

"No gompas today?"

"Not today. And we are now on the border with Kashmir, where most of the population are Muslims, so I am afraid this will be the last Tibetan Buddhist Gompa that you will visit".

I looked back at Lamayuru and was overwhelmed with sadness; to think that I would never experience anything like that again was very upsetting.

The roads were better and we managed to travel at a good speed; not that you can ever go too fast in an old jeep, but at least we were moving all the time. The air was getting slightly warmer and the vegetation was changing; it was a lot greener. We stopped in the middle of nowhere and Stanzin got off the jeep.

"Come with me, Miss Gaby, and I'll show you the rock paintings; look there", and he pointed at a stone with some primitive paintings. We kept walking and soon lots appeared, just there exposed to the elements; it was quite surreal that such magnificent paintings were just there with no protection at all. We just walked around them trying to make up what they were.

We kept on going in the jeep for a short while until we stopped at a hamlet; each house had a vegetable garden and between each house, there were lots of apricot trees.

"We are staying here tonight in a homestay, Miss Gaby; there are no guesthouses around here and I just want to show you the mill where they make the apricot oil and the Shilajit", said Stanzin, while I started to take my bags out from the jeep.

"Just take what you need for tonight, Miss Gaby; there are no thieves here in Harkun. I want to show you this place so you can see what real community living is like, just as we saw in Likhir too. Everyone here has a vegetable patch and care for some of the apricot trees; they all take the harvest to the mill and all pack the oil and share their vegetable produce. Anything left is taken to be sold in Srinagar; the oil is taken to a cooperative where is all sold at the same price; there is no haggling here and if you are caught selling it at a cheaper price, you will not be allowed to trade anymore".

"What a good idea Stanzin, so there is no haggling and no arguing".

"You can see that there are no locks in any of the doors. Children here are free to run around but they all attend a local school where they learn to read and write and basic maths. When they are 10 years old, they go to a proper school about an hour from here; but they all help with the harvest since a very young age".

"Why can't we all live like this?"

We arrived at a mudbrick house at the top of the hill; we entered and it smelt wonderful; there was a wooden stove in the middle of the room and lots of people sitting around it.

"Julley, Julley", Stanzin hugged everyone and introduced me to all.

"Julley, Julley, welcome, welcome", everyone seemed so happy to see Stanzin and me. I was taken to a small room at the back of the house. I left my things there and I joined them all for supper.

"We will go to the mill first thing in the morning, Miss Gaby. Better go to sleep now, as tomorrow will be a very long drive".

My room was small but cosy, and the bathroom was spotless clean but there was no hot running water; the lady of the house brought me a small jug with warm water and I cleaned as best I could, as I was not taking a shower in the freezing waters.

I was woken up by Stanzin knocking at my door.

"Julley, Miss Gaby; are you okay? It's getting a bit late".

I looked at my watch and it was nearly 9am.

"I'll be out in a minute; sorry Stanzin I overslept". I quickly got dressed and went out of my bedroom. "Sorry, sorry Stanzin, I don't think I've slept this well in a long time; it's so quiet here".

"It's good you had a good rest, Miss Gaby, but please hurry; we have lots to see today".

There was a pot with chai tea and bread on the table, but there was no one left in the house. I quickly had some and we left. We walked along the narrow country lanes, until we reached the mill, a very large building next to the river. Inside there were lots of people working, some filling the bottles and others sticking the labels, and placing them into boxes. They were all happily singing immersed in their jobs.

"All the bottles and labels and packaging's are supplied by the cooperative; they come and collect them twice a week", explained Stanzin. We walked into another room where there was a small shop, where visitors like me could buy the oil and Shilajit.

"Stanzin, where does the Shilajit comes from and how do they make it?"

"It comes from up high in the mountains; I have no idea how they extract it but here you can buy the best quality Shilajit".

I bought a couple of large jars of oil for me to take back to the UK and a small one to use while I was in India, and I also bought a few packets of Shilajit. Back in the jeep, I was glad to see that my luggage was all still intact. Stanzin looked at me and I just gave a big sight.

"I told you there was nothing to worry about here".

We headed back to the main road on our way to Srinagar.

"We will go as far as a nice modern hotel by the side of the road to sleep and will arrive tomorrow to Srinagar; there is only one more pass to cross in the mountains. There is a lot of military presence as we are very close to the border with Pakistan but don't worry about it; it will be okay".

"I worry when people say that everything is going to be okay because most probably, things are not okay".

"Things are a bit tense in this area, but they have been since the British divided us all up; so the chances that after so many years something is going to happen just today are very slim".

"I see your point".

We reached a roadblock; the military personnel were mostly wearing turbans and were much taller. Clearly, we were in a different territory as we crossed into Kashmir.

"Passport, please". I handed my passport to the officer and he kept looking and looking at me; Stanzin got off the jeep and left me alone with that beast of a man, that would not say nothing else. I heard them searching everything at the back of the jeep.

"This is not the place for you to be travelling alone". He handed me back my passport. "You can go now" and made a signal for Stanzin to get back on the jeep and move on.

"What was that all about Stanzin?"

"I told you things are a bit tense around here, but I think the officer fancied you".

"Men will be men, even on the rooftop of the world".

After the roadblock, we started to go downhill; we passed many military convoys, some even with tanks. It was very scary, not just because of their presence but also having to overtake them in the highest precipices in the world.

I welcomed the overnight stay only to continue travelling until we finally reached Srinagar. The entrance to the city was very chaotic. Seeing all the madness of traffic and noise again just like in Delhi was dreadful; Stanzin looking at the expression on my face, held my hand.

"I could never live in a place like this", he said.

"Where do you live Stanzin?"

"I live in the Zansker valley; it's hidden in the middle of the Himalayas, not far from Rangoon, we passed quite close to it".

"Why didn't we go?"

"Accessing it is quite difficult; the pass isn't always open. After I drop you at the airport I will buy my supplies and head straight there; if I leave it too long I won't be able to go there until the spring. It's very beautiful but very cold and there is no internet connexion; but I think you would like the Gompa; not many people ever go there and the monks are truly enlightened".

"Promise me you will take me to visit your home next time I come to India".

"I hope one day you will come back, Miss Gaby, and I promise you I will take you to meet my family".

"I hope so too Stanzin".

Srinagar also known as the Venice of the East, lies in the Kashmir Valley on the banks of the Jhelum River. The city is surrounded by two lakes, the Dal Lake and the Nigeen Lake. We were going to stay in one of the famous houseboats on the banks of the Dal Lake. We arrived at the waterfront and there was the most beautiful wooden houseboat; a man came to greet us and we all walked across a narrow plank into the boat. I was pleasantly surprised to see how lavishly decorated the houseboat was, with chandeliers hanging from the ceiling, oriental carpets covering the floors and it was furnished with French style sofas and a dining table; it looked like a stately home floating on the lake. The views across the lake took my breath away, with the sun just about to set, creating a golden reflection of the small boats floating by. I was taken to my room and the owner gave me the password for the internet.

"Did I hear well; you have internet connection here in the boat?"

"Of course, we have. At what time do you want dinner?"

"7 pm is fine".

I went out and told Stanzin to meet me early the following morning. I was going to try and book my return flight to London and rest after the long day travelling.

I opened my emails and had a quick look but not one email from Wagner, nothing. I wondered if I had given him my correct email address but I thought I would wait until London before writing to him or anyone else. I booked my return flight home; I would stay three more days in Srinagar before flying to Delhi, connecting from there to London. It took me a while before I could press the button confirming the purchase. I felt so sad; it had been such a wonderful experience and I did not want it to end; reluctantly I pressed the button. I forwarded the details to Linda and turned off my mobile.

Early next morning I had breakfast with Stanzin, while we planned the few days ahead. I was going to cross the lake that morning in a shikara, and see the floating markets of the lake and he would be waiting for me at the other side, so we could go and find Jesus' tomb.

A shikara, or small wooden boat, was waiting for me next to the houseboat; I boarded it and a very pleasant young man sitting at the end of it started rowing and the boat moved slowly, gliding through the lake waters. We later entered into a more secluded area that was covered with gigantic water lilies with lots of pink and blue flowers and amongst them lots of birds. The wind and sun were caressing my face and I just closed my eyes dreaming that I could stay there forever. Soon I was woken up of my day dreaming by lots of other boats approaching; they were selling all sorts of things, from vegetable, to flowers and of course beautiful Kashmir scarfs. I fell into temptation and bought some colourful ones that would probably look a treat in London and maybe I would have to wear them all on my flight back home as I wasn't sure if they would fit in my already jam-packed luggage.

Stanzin was waiting for me at the other side of the lake; I would miss that beautiful smile of his, always wanting to please me.

"Julley, Julley. Miss Gaby, we can go now to the Rozabal shrine, it's in one of the backstreets not too far from here, but you have to dress up as a Muslim if you want to go inside; the people around the shrine don't like tourists visiting, and they don't allow anyone to take photographs or videos".

"Better take me to a street market where I can buy a cheap tunic and hijab".

Stanzin found a good market and I just bought the largest tunic so it would cover me all up. I dressed in the jeep and we then drove towards the shrine. I felt sad having to cover my face with the hijab and having to glance at the world through the small opening between my eyes. I can't imagine what it must be like for the Muslim women that have to wear it all their lives. It took us quite a long time to get there, due to the traffic and bad condition of the roads. I was quite disappointed when we finally reached the tomb, to see such a small and insignificant building right across a cemetery but my heart was pounding just thinking that Jesus might be buried there. Stanzin asked me to wait in the jeep; he talked to a local couple that agreed to take me in for a few rupees; he thought it was better if I didn't go in all by myself. They told me that two great prophets were buried there: Yuz Asif, which in Hebrew is Jesus, together with another Muslim holy man. They also told me that there was a rock carving of feet bearing crucifixion wounds and that the body was buried according to Jewish traditions and not according to the Islamic tradition. We all went in quietly and I prayed by the grave. I soon started to cry; there was a very special energy in that place, whether it was really Jesus buried in there I wasn't sure but I did feel something very special being there. I thought that if indeed he was buried there, the greatest man that have ever walked on this earth, was born a Jew, the catholic church was created because of him and he was buried amongst Muslims. And yet, why did so many people fight because of religion? What a crazy world we were living in. I don't know how long I had spent there when other people came into the tomb and the couple quickly ushered me out. When we made it back to the jeep, I paid them and I gave the lady my clothes as I was sure I would never use them again. They had served its purpose and I was very grateful that they enabled me to go into such a special place.

We spent the last few days visiting some very beautiful gardens around Srinagar and a few stunning Hindu temples, but the one that I will never forget would be the Rozabal shrine.

Finally, it was time to say goodbye. Stanzin walked with me in the airport helping me to carry my very heavy bags and as the Air India's agent behind the counter was his friend, he did not charge me for my excess luggage. I gave him Wagner's sleeping bag, a huge tip and I hugged him so hard as I did not want to let go of the experiences he had given me during those two fantastic weeks in the Himalayas.

After a short wait at Delhi's airport, I found myself finally heading back home.

London

The pilot announced that we had to fasten our seat belts on as we were approaching Heathrow airport. I looked out my window and I started to see London's skyline appearing through the clouds; we flew over the O2 arena and then started to trail the Thames and all the famous landmarks, the Tower Bridge, the London Eye and the Houses of Parliament… Such a beautiful city and I just happened to live there. I had mixed feelings; on the one side, I was sad that such a great experience was coming to an end and on the other hand, I was really looking forward to getting back to the safe haven of my home.

There was no chaos clearing customs; just orderly long queues. After collecting all my luggage, I went out the exit doors and there amongst the crowds was Linda.

"Gaby, Gaby", she shouted calling out for me.

"Linda, so wonderful to see you. I wasn't expecting you here at the airport", I said giving her a big hug.

"You didn't think I was going to let you travel on the tube alone with all this luggage".

"Whatever the reason, I am very happy to see you".

We started walking towards the tube station; I looked around and most people were dressed in black. No colourful saris and no one said Julley, Julley as we walked past them. We English are very quiet and sombre; maybe things would soon change in cosmopolitan London, and we might become bright, spontaneous happy people, but just looking around I thought that maybe could take years…

I bought my ticket to Bayswater and it was more expensive than a full day's ride in a tuck-tuck in Delhi.

"What a rip-off", I said staring at it.

"Welcome back to expensive London".

We carried my luggage down the escalators; they were so heavy and it was such a struggle. I was really happy that Linda had come all the way to help me out. As we approached central London, the train got very crowded.

"Linda, how are we going to get out of this train and change at Earl's Court?"

"Don't panic; that's why I came to help you out".

I was very tired and just wanted to arrive home; I think I would have taken a taxi if Linda had not been waiting for me at the airport, but it was awfully nice for her to come out and help so early in the morning. When we finally made it to my tube station, we stopped at the local Costa Coffee place and I ordered my favourite cappuccino.

"Soya, decaf cappuccino with chocolate on top please", I said. We just sat there catching our breath before the final walk to my flat.

"You are looking great Gaby".

"I can't be looking great after travelling for more than fifteen hours, from Srinagar to London".

"You are glowing".

"I just want to go to bed".

"Finish your coffee and I will help you home, but I won't come in as I have to go to work".

"I hope you haven't told anyone I was arriving today; I still have another month before my sabbatical ends and I need the space for me to decide what to do with my life".

"Don't worry, I haven't told anyone that you were coming, but I will come by on Saturday and promise me you will tell me all about your adventures".

"Bring a bottle of prosecco; it's a very long story!"

After a few more yards dragging my entire luggage, we made it to my flat. I gave Linda a big hug and I stepped into my home.

The flat was immaculately clean, but it looked dark and gloomy. I opened the curtains that lead into my garden and Oh Dear me! What a terrible sight! It looked as if the Amazon jungle had moved into my back yard; it was completely overgrown, my pride and joy totally ruined. My energy totally changed; I knew I couldn't go to rest knowing the mess the garden was in. I left my luggage in my bedroom and went right back into the garden, put my gloves on and started clearing up the mess. I gathered five full black rubbish bags of garden waste; I was more than exhausted and when I caught sight of myself in the mirror I looked like a mad woman, covered in leaves and dirt, with a few scratches here and there. Now I was totally exhausted, but I felt happy; I took a long shower and collapsed in my welcoming bed.

I woke up and it was pitch black. I went to the kitchen and saw that Linda had left me a few things to eat, I made myself a coffee and a couple of toasts, went to my small office, looked for my laptop and finally I started looking at all the emails I had not opened for such a long time.

There was one from George: "Hi, gorgeous let me know when you are back in London so we can finally have a proper date". I thought about George; he had been such a wonderful companion during the Camino, and I did want to see him again; we never really had a chance to get to know each other and he was very nice and best of all he lives nearby. "Dear George, just arrived yesterday, give me a week or so and yes I would like to catch up. Love Gaby". I thought it was best to keep it short and sweet.

And one from Yousef. "Hello my love, when are you coming back to Morocco, I am waiting here for you". Deep down I knew that I would never go back there; it had been a magical few days, but not something I wanted to repeat ever again. "Dear Yousef, I only arrived yesterday from my long trip and I don't think I am ready to travel for some time just yet, love, Gaby". I just hopped he understood that going back was probably never going to happen.

And one from Anika and Dev: "We are getting married in December. If you are in India please come, we are forever grateful for what you did, we can never thank you enough". I was so happy to read that news. "Congratulations! I think the angels conspired together to make everything happen, it was absolutely magical and I am immensely happy that they chose me to make it all possible; I am also very grateful with you for introducing me to Stanzin and to the Himalayas; it was truly an experience of a lifetime; so we are even. If I don't make it to your wedding in person, rest assured that my soul will be there with you".

I replied a few more emails from friends and from Tom, my boss, telling them I was okay and would be arriving in a months' time; otherwise, they would all be wanting to see me and I wasn't ready to face anyone just yet. And as I was about to close my laptop an email from Wagner came in. "Let me know when you get back from India so I can call you and we can talk". I thought about it for a while: there was no, I've missed you, love you, ore any sign of any kind of feelings at all. I just closed my laptop quite disappointed, not replying anything at all.

I stared to my now bare garden; I wanted to create my own sanctuary and recreate the Lichi Verdi meditation space in Ranchi, underneath my lovely oak tree. I looked at my watch and it was still too early to go out and buy anything, so I unpacked my bags and placed all the ornaments I had bought around my flat. I sat down and looked around; it was already starting to feel more like home, and more like the new me.

I went out to the nearest garden centre and bought some plants, not many as autumn was approaching but I did buy the biggest Buddha I could find and lots of bulbs so that I could have a very colourful spring. Once I placed it all, I sat under the tree and dreamt that I was still in the Himalayas meditating with the monks. Now I truly had a sanctuary in my own back garden. I had never felt so much at peace in all my life; after all that travelling I had come to realize that there is no place like home and the only travelling we really need to do is right inside within our soul and only there we can truly find that peace that we all crave for.

There was just one more thing for me to do and that was to pay a visit to my hairdresser.

"Hello, Gaby, lovely to see you, when did you come back?"

"Two days ago. I still have jetlag but I needed to come and see you".

"Let me take a good look at your hair. OMG, what do you want me to do?; chop it all off? And those nai-ls, did you want to join the cast of the Monster Family or what?"

"This is what happens when I don't come and see you for a long time. But I trust you can sort me out today before I see any of my friends".

"Besides your hair and nails, you are looking great. So after today you can go down the pub and I am sure you won't come out from there alone".

"Those days are over, Jackie".

"Don't tell me you are going to become an old age pensioner already?"

"Hahahaha, not yet but I'm not doing one night stands anymore".

Jackie just looked at me and laughed.

"Better pass me a Hello magazine so can I get up to date on the royals and showbiz world".

After a long afternoon I came out looking gorgeous; I was even tempted to wander to Soho and my old hunting grounds, but thought better not fall into temptation.

Linda came by on Saturday with a couple of bottles of prosecco,

"I came well prepared; this is going to be a very long night as you must tell me absolutely everything".

I told her all about the Camino and George and Portugal and Fátima, Málaga and Richard, Morocco and Yousef; I told her about my near-death experience in Istanbul and India and the Himalayas and Wagner.

"OMG and what are you going to do?"

"If you are thinking about your job, don't worry I don't think I can go back to the same routine".

"I am not worried about my job; Tom is thinking of giving you a more prominent position. He realizes now that he hasn't treated you the way that you deserve; maybe you can find your balance between your job and this new more meaningful life you have discovered".

"I'm not sure, Linda. I would soon find myself submerged in work and this new meaningful life would be forgotten. Tom has always known that he wasn't treating me right and he is just afraid to lose me and probably worse, having to pay my redundancy money".

"So how are you planning to support yourself?"

"I trust the universe will show me the way".

"You better tell the universe what you want; otherwise the universe won't know what to give you", Linda said looking straight into my eyes and I immediately changed the subject.

"Now, tell me all about you and your boys".

"We better leave that for another day. I have to go now, as the boys will wake up soon wanting breakfast", Linda said looking at the time; it was past midnight and she was looking rather tired.

I went to bed thinking about what Linda had said, and she was right: I needed to know what I wanted and ask the universe to point me in the right direction.

It was a crisp sunny morning and I took my matt and placed it on the decking in the garden. As I was preparing myself to start doing some yoga and meditation, I heard my neighbour calling me.

"Morning, Gaby; nice to see your back. You mind if I join you?"

"Please do, but bring a matt".

Lucy lived just above me and we had greeted every time we saw each other but nothing more than that, so I was very surprised to hear that she wanted to come down and do yoga with me. When she came in and we did a few yoga postures or asanas and then lit some incenses and a candle and I guided her in a meditation, with the beautiful chant of a black bird singing in the distance, that made it quite magical.

"Gaby, that was absolutely wonderful; have you ever considered teaching? I can bring some of my friends and we can always pay you".

"I never thought about it, but we can always give it a try".

"How about tomorrow at 7am before we all go to work?"

We agreed, I gave her a hug and I just sat there and thanked the universe because it was definitely guiding me towards the future I wanted for myself.

The following morning it was very wet and windy. I quickly moved all the furniture in the lounge and made room for my clients. I placed all the Indian artefacts around the place, lit candles, incense, deemed the lights and ding-dong, they arrived. Lucy my neighbour was standing at the door with two of her friends; they all looked happy coming in. I put some soft music and started the class; we did the yoga and finished the meditation with the sound of my Tibetan tingsha bells. They were very happy and asked me if they could bring more friends. I said I could have maximum six in my lounge; only if the weather was good we could move into the garden.

Sure enough, there were six ladies standing at the door the following morning and that is how my school of yoga and meditation started.

Travelling in a jam-packed rush hour train back to my old work place to meet my boss, helped me confirm that the decision to hand in my notice was the correct one. Nevertheless, I was nervous. Standing up to Tom was never easy; he always had a way of convincing me that he was right and I was wrong. As I entered to office lots of my colleagues came to greet me.

"Look at you, looking more fabulous than ever".

"You could be the face of our next cosmetic advertising campaign"

"Please stop it, you are making me blush; but for the record, this I all natural, there is no Botox that can ever compare with beauty that comes within".

Linda came to my rescue:

"Come on, Gaby. Tom is waiting for you".

"See you all later; maybe me can all go after work to The French House", I said as I walked to Tom's office.

"Please come on in, sit down, welcome back" said Tom looking at me from head to toe. I sat in front of him feeling like a schoolgirl in the headmaster's office about to be told off.

"I am sure that Linda already told you that I am planning to make you a director of the whole department and increase your salary by 5%. I also intend to give you the office next to Linda's as Peter is leaving us at the end of the month and I trust you will come back to full time work by then; although you can come back now and share your old office with Linda as you are quite close", said Tom in a very confident tone as if his proposal was already a done deal.

"Sorry, Tom, but I am not coming back; I am here to hand in my notice and to work out with HR my redundancy package, as I trust you will pay me in full what is owed to me".

"What! After all these years and such a generous offer, you are leaving? What, is it you want more money?"

"No, Tom; it is not about the money; is about what I want to do for the rest of my life, and being buried here working all hours of the day and night is not the future I want for myself", I said very posed and relaxed.

"You are telling me that giving a few yoga lessons to your friends will pay the bills and make you happy for the rest of your life?"

"I am not here to discuss my future life with you; I am here to tell you that this one right here is coming to an end today, and there is nothing you can say or do to convince me otherwise". Tom was now looking livid; he did not know what to say, clearly things were not going his way and he was not happy about it.

"You want some time to think things through. I can increase your salary up to 8%"

"I don't need more time, and it's not about the money; I am going to spend the day in HR and clearing all my things; you can join us after work in the pub if you want to".

"I am really going to miss you", Tom said, finally conceding

"Thanks for everything Tom, I am very grateful for all these years of putting up with me. And please don't make Linda work late every day; she has two young boys waiting for her at home". I gave him a big hug and left.

Later in the pub, I told everyone I was leaving and they all joked about it, saying that they all thought the only way I was ever going to leave that job was in a coffin.

"Well, I proved you all wrong, didn't I? Cheers". I toasted, put my glass down and left.

That evening at home with a few prosecco's in my head I finally had the courage to reply to Wagner. I now knew that as idyllic as the few days of romance in the Himalayas had been, I would never leave home and move to Germany but I hoped we could remain good friends for ever.

So, that only left George. I invited him out to dinner. I wanted to look good, sexy, but not too sensual. I tried just about everything in my wardrobe and thought how easy it had been in the Camino when I only had one dress and he didn't even mind. I finally put on a short red dress with black stilettoes and one of my new beautiful pashminas. I heard the doorbell rang; I looked at my watch and thought that he was rather early. But when I opened the door, I was very surprised to see Peter, my last toy-boy lover.

"Hello, beautiful".

"What on earth are you doing here?"

"As you never returned my calls, I thought I better come and pay you a visit. But let me look at you; I must have been mad for ever leaving you"

Sorry, Peter, but there is a gentleman waiting for me in his car", I said to him as I saw George arriving in a convertible car.

"Where are you going?"

"Machu Picchu!"